The Torc and the Ring

The Torc and the Ring

Margaret Joy

faber and faber
LONDON · BOSTON

First published in 1996
by Faber and Faber Limited
3 Queen Square London WC1N 3AU

Typeset by Faber and Faber Limited
Printed in England by Clays Ltd, St Ives plc

© Margaret Joy, 1996

A CIP record for this book
is available from the British Library

ISBN 0–571–17806–5

2 4 6 8 10 9 7 5 3 1

Contents

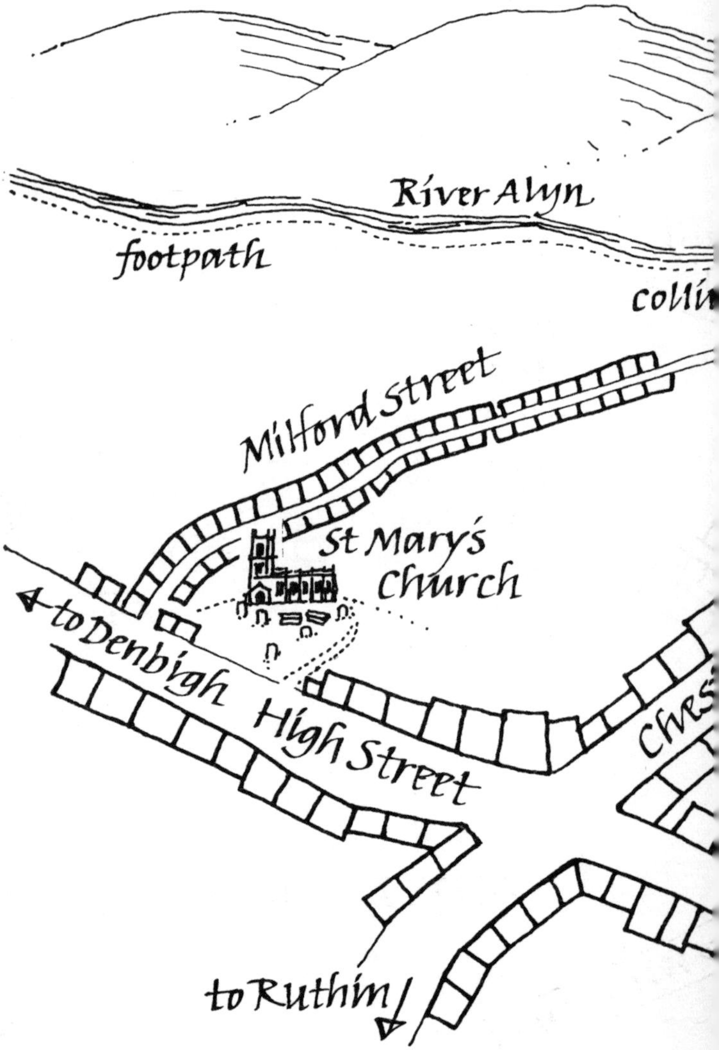

River Alyn
footpath
colli
Milford Street
St Mary's Church
to Denbigh
High Street
Ches
to Ruthin

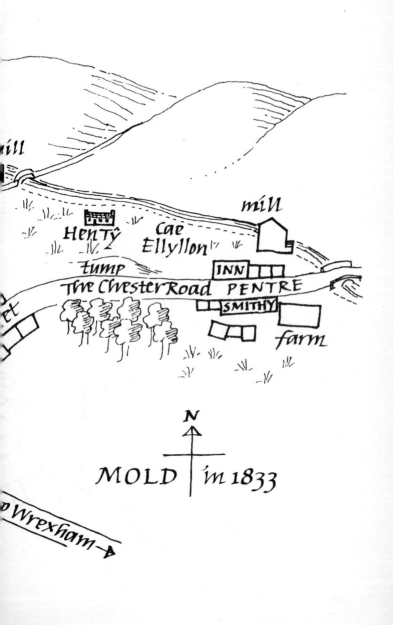

ill

mill

Hen Tŷ

Cae
Ellyllon

tump

The Chester Road   PENTRE

INN

SMITHY

farm

N

MOLD in 1833

Wrexham →

Mold, North Wales

This Year

William was woken by the smell of frying bacon. He pulled the sheet away from his face and breathed in deeply. Mmmm – this was how the first minutes of his birthday always smelt. He lay for a moment, smiling to himself, then shot out of bed. He dressed and went down the stairs two at a time and into the kitchen.

Jet came trotting over wagging her tail in greeting. William's mum was sitting reading a letter with a preoccupied frown. She looked up and saw him. Her expression brightened. She stuffed the letter into her handbag and pointed to two parcels on the table.

'Happy birthday, William,' she said. She gave his shoulders a quick squeeze.

'I hope they're what you asked for,' she said. 'I went to Wheelies and they were very helpful.'

William pulled the paper and string off the largest parcel. Inside was a pair of green waterproof panniers for his bike.

'Oh, great,' he beamed. 'I'll be able to carry no end in these.'

In the next parcel was a cycling helmet. The padding was made of white polystyrene, and the straps were purple and blue. William's eyes lit up. He perched the helmet on top of his thick black hair. Jet barked in surprise.

'Thanks, Mum, they're ace,' exclaimed William. He was delighted. Things had been so tight, he had thought his mum wouldn't manage anything for his birthday.

'Now eat your butty while it's hot,' said his mother. 'And then have some cornflakes or toast or something.'

She inspected her face in the mirror.

'I must dash. Now have I got everything? – handbag, money, door key. Right. Have a good day, love. Don't forget to take your trunks for swimming practice this afternoon. I'll see you after school. I'll bring in a birthday cake and something nice for tea.'

'Bye, Mum.'

William made some toast and investigated the panniers. He'd organize them at the weekend. He still had the new helmet on. He did up the straps; it felt really comfortable. He heard the letter-box flapping – must be the postie.

He went to look – six cards to open. He stood them next to the king-size one his mum had given him. And there was a small padded envelope too.

'Who's this from?' William turned it over. His name and address were written in bold black felt-tip letters.

'Great-grandfather.'

His dad's grandfather. Even though his dad had walked out, the old man always remembered. He had a good memory for dates. He was nearly ninety and lived in an old people's flat down in London, but he'd been born and brought up in Mold, like William.

Inside the envelope, something was wrapped in a piece of bubble-packing. It felt like a bullet. William unrolled it.

'Wow – a Swiss army knife – *wicked*!'

William could hardly believe it. He had always longed to have one of these, but they were far too expensive. It weighed down his palm, shiny, dark red, with all sorts

4

of secret blades layered inside it. He picked up the piece of paper and frowned over the thick black writing.

Dear William,

I think you're old enough to have one of these. But take care, it's meant for a Swiss soldier, so it's *very sharp*! Don't go fooling about with it.
Love,

Yr. Gt. Grandfather.

Good for Great-grandfather!

William was glad his mother had already left for work. He had a feeling she wouldn't approve of this present. He pushed his thumb-nail into the little groove in one of the blades and pulled it out. His toast was ready, so he spread margarine and marmalade across it with the blade of the knife, then cut the toast into thin fingers; it was as easy as parting water.

William wiped the blade clean with his hanky. Then he pulled out the tiny scissors and cut across the padded envelope – fantastic – the blades were sharp as razors. All the padding came out and fell on the table like grey dust. William bent down and blew it away, but it stuck to the marge and the marmalade.

He glanced at the clock. Better get going. He wiped the shining blades once more and put the knife in his pocket. He shooed Jet outside into the back garden and filled the bowl in her kennel with water.

Then he wheeled his bike outside, made sure he had the key on the string round his neck and slammed the door behind him.

He cycled down the road to school, and was just pad-locking his bike when the bell went.

At playtime he brought the penknife out again. Everyone gathered round. He opened all the blades and gadgets to show them off. Lindy Lassiter peered at it.

'Is it sharp?' she asked.

''Course it is,' said William. 'It'd be no good if Swiss soldiers carried round blunt knives, would it?'

'Oh, William, that's dangerous,' breathed Melanie, wide-eyed. Lindy took no notice of her friend.

'Show us then,' she urged. 'Go on, show us.'

William felt uncomfortable; under that tangled fringe there was a gleam in Lassie's eyes that seemed to be forcing him to do something. A crowd was gathering, all staring at the new knife. William looked round for something to cut. Behind him was the classroom win-dowsill, made of wood. Everyone pressed closer to see. There was a sudden hush.

William pushed a shining blade point into the green paintwork. A deep white line appeared. Some of the spectators gasped. He pulled the knife point across – that was a bit harder. But he had cut a good L.

'See?' he said to Lindy Lassiter. 'I've done an L – easy-peasy.'

'That's not much,' she said scornfully. 'Do all my name.'

'Yeah,' they all urged him on. 'Go on, William, do her name.'

It was easy enough. William scratched another down-stroke for a capital I. The N was downstrokes too. The first part of the D was easy.

But then he tried to pull the point of the blade round in a nice smooth curve. This was much harder. He put his tongue between his teeth to help him concentrate. He began to sweat.

'William Bellis!'

'Aahhh! – Old Fishy!'

The knife slipped and notched the side of William's finger. Everyone had scattered as Mr Salmon came up to them. His eyes widened as he saw

LIND

scratched in white letters in the green windowsill. A white-faced William stood alone with the penknife in one hand and blood dripping from the other.

2

The rest of the class had scattered across the playground, pretending they hadn't been anywhere near. Mr Salmon just stood there, silent, hands on hips, lips pressed tightly together. William wished he would at least say *some*thing.

Then he did. He really let rip – a whole lot of stuff about school property and vandalism and brainless idiots. He said it all very quietly indeed, but the air was sizzling. William could feel his heart pounding; his legs felt like jelly.

Then Mr Salmon pulled a clean hanky out of his

pocket and wound it tight round William's finger.

'You'll live,' he said icily. 'And whoever gave a boy your age a dangerous weapon like that must have been out of their mind. They want their head examined. Who was it?'

'My great-grandfather, s-sir,' stammered William.

'Your what?' Mr Salmon stared disbelievingly.

'He's eighty-nine.'

'Well, at his age he ought to know better then!' snorted Mr Salmon.

He held out his hand. There was nothing William could do. He slowly placed the precious red knife in Mr Salmon's outstretched palm.

'*I'll* be looking after that for a while,' he said, 'and if your great-grandfather raises any objections, send him to me.'

He looked at the windowsill again, then at William.

'Come to the staffroom after lunch, and I'll tell you what to do while the others go for swimming practice.'

'Swimming practice? Oh, but sir –'

'You don't really think I'd let you go swimming while this mess needs seeing to?'

'But sir – you already made me miss five-a-side last week!'

'*I* made you miss, William … ? There was the small matter of a whole morning wrestling with one sum, remember?'

'Oh, but sir, that's not fair – I've got to practise with the team. I'm down for the fifty metres in the Gala – oh, sir – *please*, sir …'

But Mr Salmon shook his head.

8

'No, William,' he said firmly. 'No swimming practice. Come to me at twelve-thirty.'

William couldn't believe it. Why did these things always happen to him?

At twelve-thirty, Mr Salmon began to instruct William how to use glass-paper and plastic wood filler to bring the surface of the windowsill back to normal.

'Tomorrow you can paint it over,' said Mr Salmon. 'That should take care of the next swimming practice.'

'Oh, but *sir* –'

At that moment the rest of the class filed past with their sports bags, on their way to the baths. Most of them looked sympathetic. But Lindy Lassiter poked her pointy nose at William and shouted: 'Aren't you coming with us then, William?'

'Oh, shurrup, Lassie,' growled some of the others.

'Yeah, shurrrup, Lassie,' they scowled at her.

William said nothing. But he could have kicked her. Hard.

Later, Mr Salmon inspected the work. William had sandpapered it down to raw wood. At least that beastly Lindy's name had disappeared; she really was the Pain of all Pains. William wondered what had come over him.

Mr Salmon ran his hand along the bare wood. 'Smooth enough,' he grunted. 'Right, William, come into the art room.'

He led the way.

'I'm tidying up the stock cupboard while the others are out.' He glanced at his watch. 'You can spend the last half hour here.'

He gave William a large sheet of paper and a piece of charcoal.

'Here, draw what you like.'

The creamy paper was thick, with a bumpy sort of surface. This was a real treat; William loved drawing. He put his tongue between his teeth and began to concentrate. He forgot about Old Fishy, and the knife, and his birthday, and Lindy Beastly Lassiter. With quick sketching movements he drew his precious bike, going at speed, then a couple of others half a wheel behind him, pedalling madly to catch up. The charcoal was rather smudgy, but William was really pleased with it.

His hands were black. He wiped them on his hanky which already seemed to have grease all over it. He shrugged and stuffed it back in his pocket. The bell went. Mr Salmon came out from the depths of the stock room. He stared at William's picture.

'Can I go, sir?'

'Go? Oh, yes, yes,' he said, his eyes still on the picture.

William picked up his bag and shot out of the room as fast as he could. At the bike shed he undid his padlock, strapped on his helmet, and slung his bag across his chest. He decided to go home through Tesco's car park. It was very quiet at the far end by the bottle banks.

The wall gleamed almost white in the sunshine. It looked very inviting. Something came over William again. He leaned his bike against the wall. The week before, he had been respraying a scratch on the mudguard, and the tin of red spray paint was still in his saddlebag. Now he pulled it out.

It took him about two minutes to sketch a large dog

with long fur. Its face looked definitely human, with a tangled fringe and a long pointy nose. She was easy to recognize. William wrote underneath:

Lassie go home!

It was really good. He stepped back to look at it. He hardly noticed a woman trudging past pushing a pram.

But he felt amazingly better. He cycled home in high spirits.

$$\underline{\underline{3}}$$

William let himself in the front, then Jet in the back. Everything was just as he had left it. He had half an hour before his mother arrived home.

First he fed Jet. Then he began to clear up the table. He took the bits of padded bag and hid them in the dustbin. Then he scraped most of the grey dust off the margarine. He blew at the sugar bowl; the grey speckles, and quite a bit of the sugar too, shot into the air. But at least they had gone.

He washed up quickly. What about Old Fishy's hanky? He couldn't very well throw it away. There were large patches of blood on it; it had to be washed. And there was his own greasy grey hanky too.

William pushed them to the back of the washer and mixed them up well with some of the other bits of dirty washing. His mother was amazingly terrier-like. Anything out of the ordinary and she would worry at it like a knot in her knitting until it was unravelled.

But on this occasion, William reckoned he'd managed pretty well. She'd never suspect a thing. He heard her key in the lock and suddenly felt rather nervous.

'Yoo-oo. William? I'm back.'

His mum sailed in and dumped several carrier bags on the floor of the kitchen.

'How's my birthday boy then?' She gave William an enormous bear hug. 'Nice day at school?'

William suddenly wanted to tell her everything. He searched for the right words. But she was already going on. ' … Just give me a hand with all this shopping; we're going to have the biggest feast since your last birthday.'

It was a good meal too, all William's favourites – tinned tomato soup, bangers and mash and mushy peas, finished off with ice-cream gâteau and sherry trifle. He began to feel much better. But then mum got up to put the kettle on. That was when things started going wrong again. She suddenly peered down at the floor.

'D'you know, it's a funny thing,' she said, 'I keep hearing crunching noises when I walk. I wonder what it is …'

She peered even more closely at the floor.

'Oh – it's sugar. I don't remember spilling any sugar. William –'

At that moment the phone rang. Mum went to answer it. William sighed with relief. But he shouldn't have done.

'Oh – Grandfather!' exclaimed his mother. She waved an arm at William and hissed, 'It's Grandfather.'

Pause. She looked round the room, then answered:

'No, nothing's arrived yet.'

William avoided her eye. Pause. She shook her head and tutted.

'Yes, the post's getting worse all the time, isn't it?'

Pause.

'My goodness, those were the days, weren't they?' Mum rolled her eyes at William. 'A penny – is that all it cost?

'Well, I'm sure he'll write and thank you when it arrives. What is it anyway?'

William held his breath.

'A secret? Oh, I won't spoil the surprise then. Bye, Grandfather ...'

She turned from the phone to find William crouched on the floor, brushing the sugar into a dustpan.

'Guess what,' she said. 'Grandfather's sending you a surprise present. He's a marvel for nearly ninety. I wonder what it is.'

William smiled weakly. He went into the kitchen and emptied the brushed up sugar into the waste-bin. Then he went into the hall and began to busy himself with the bike. Mum bustled to and fro, humming as she cleared up in the kitchen. When he realized that the humming had stopped, he knew there was something up.

'William ...? Your swimming things aren't wet. Didn't you go swimming this afternoon?'

'No.' That was true.

'Did the others go?'

'Yes.' That was true too. So far so good. But she was beginning to suspect.

'So why were you left behind?'

'I stayed with Mr Salmon. He was clearing out the stock cupboard.'

That, too, was true, but Mum was immediately indignant.

'He shouldn't make you miss swimming to help him do that!'

William drew a deep breath. Why were simple things so tricky?

'It's all right, Mum. I didn't mind.'

'Well, I think it's all wrong,' she said crossly. 'I don't send you to school to help clear out cupboards. If that's what you want, I can always find you cupboards here at home …'

'Oh, *Mum* …'

She bent down and began to sort out the washing. The air was suddenly still again. William picked up the lead, clipped it onto Jet's collar and tiptoed towards the door.

'William? What's this hanky doing here? It's covered in blood. What've you been doing?'

'Nothing really. Mr Salmon let me borrow it. I just cut my finger a bit …'

Mum came into the hall and stood over William, holding out the red-splashed hanky by its two top corners. She suddenly reminded him of a bullfighter.

'Olé!'

'Don't joke with me, William Bellis,' she said. 'You're just trying to cover up for that man. I'm going up to the school to see him. He has no right to make you clear out filthy old cupboards with rough edges, then just give you an old hanky to mop up your blood, when he

14

should have taken you straight to first aid. You might have needed stitches.'

She put her hands on her hips.

'Show me the cut,' she demanded.

William showed her his left forefinger.

'William!' she exclaimed. 'You should have a plaster on that. Go to the bathroom and get one this instant. And I'll go up to school tomorrow and have a word with that Mr Salmon …'

'Oh, Mum, no …'

William's heart sank at the thought of such public embarrassment. He said desperately: 'Look, I'll sort it out.'

'It's that man that wants sorting out,' Mum said indignantly.

'No, leave it, Mum, please leave it. Look, I'll talk to you after. Me and Jet are just going along the river for a bit.'

At last they were outside. Jet pulled eagerly to the end of Milford Street, then they crossed the main road and hurried down to the Alyn. The hills formed a green bowl round the town, through which the little river flowed.

Only when they were well along the towpath did William slow down. He let Jet off the lead and she raced off into the fields. The Alyn here was little more than a stream trickling over pebbles. William found an old tyre and threw it into the middle. Then he pulled a large rock down the bank and pushed it into the water to make another stepping-stone. He picked his way across the stream, holding onto a willow branch at the other side to help him balance. He suddenly lurched.

'Ouch – oh, *spit.*' A shoe was full of water.

He hobbled back to the bank and sat down to shake

his shoe. He tried to dry it out with handfuls of grass and yellow ragwort. The light was unusual – half day, half dusk. The sun was setting in a blaze of orange and gold which lit up the sky in brilliant streaks.

'Jet? Jet, where are you?'

William whistled. Jet came bounding back and stopped a metre away. Eyes bright with excitement, she bent her head and dropped something, tail wagging furiously, panting with triumph. William picked up the bone she'd dropped and shied it away across the stream.

'Don't go digging up old sheep, stupid,' he said. 'Go on, find something over there in the bank.'

The collie plunged into the water and splashed across to the far bank, where she began to sniff at holes under the willow roots.

Something made William look over his shoulder. His breath suddenly stopped.

Framed against the trees in a bend of the Alyn was the figure of a man. Caught in the unearthly light of the setting sun, his shoulders and chest shone with a dazzling golden light. For a second or two he moved soundlessly up the field past the Old House towards Pentre. Then he was gone.

4

'But it *was* a man, Mum, I'm sure it was – a man in gold, all shining –'

'That's what sherry trifle does …'

'No, Mum, honest, I'm not joking.'

'I believe you, love, I believe you. But it was probably just someone out with his dog, like you, and there was a trick of the light … Did you see the wonderful sunset?'

'Well, yes …'

'There you are, you see – it was the sunset dazzling you.' Mum smiled triumphantly.

'Yes … but …' The picture of the golden figure was imprinted on William's memory. He knew he hadn't imagined it.

'Anyway, forget it for now. I've got something I want to talk to you about.'

Mum suddenly seemed preoccupied. William's heart sank. Old Fishy hadn't been on the phone, had he?

'What's the matter?' he asked nervously.

'Come and sit down,' Mum said.

That sounded serious. It must be leading up to a talking-to. William sat on the edge of his chair.

'I'm sorry to mention this on your birthday, but I think you're old enough now to understand certain things.'

It *must* be Old Fishy.

'It's this house,' Mum said.

'Oh, the *house* …' said William.

He sat back more comfortably.

'It's too big for just the two of us. When your dad left, I said I would never give up the house, but the bills are getting too much – electricity, gas, repairs to the roof; the place needs painting, and the brickwork needs repointing; I can't go on pouring money into this place – there's nothing left over for ourselves.'

William shook his head sympathetically.

'And now the interest rate has gone up again, so my repayments are really more than I can manage.'

What was she getting at?

'So?' he prompted.

'So, I think we should move,' she said.

'Oh, is that all?' said William.

'Don't you mind?' Mum said in surprise.

'Where are we moving to?'

'Somewhere in Mold, but cheaper. I don't want you to move from your school.'

'Oh, that's all right then,' said William.

'So I'll put this house up for sale,' said his mother, 'and we'll go house-hunting.'

'Me too?'

'Yes, of course. I want you to like the new place too.'

'Oh, great.' That sounded like fun. 'Perhaps we could live by the swimming baths or the rugby field?'

His mother laughed. She was looking happier now. She changed the subject.

'I wonder what your great-grandfather's mystery present will be.'

'Mmmm,' said William vaguely. He edged away, 'I think there's something on telly I've been waiting to see, Mum …'

Next day was Thursday. William shot off to school, not giving his mother a chance to say anything about her visit to Mr Salmon. In fact, she had decided to let the matter drop, but thought it would do no harm to let William stay on pins about it – just for a while …

But for William there was no avoiding Old Fishy – he was in the corridor waiting. He came straight to the point.

'Did you have a tin of red spray paint yesterday, William?'

William stared at him and swallowed hard. He could feel his cheeks burning.

'Did you spray something on the wall of Tesco's car park?'

How did he know that? William still couldn't say a word. Mr Salmon's expression showed he was determined to find out the truth.

'My wife happened to be passing and saw someone very like you.'

The woman with the pram. Of course.

'*Lassie go home*,' went on Mr Salmon. 'Lindy Lassiter, I suppose.'

William looked at his feet. He was very close to giggling. Or crying.

'Do you deny it?'

William shook his head.

'Right,' said Mr Salmon, 'then when you've finished painting the windowsill this afternoon, I'll get a tin of graffiti removal from the caretaker, and you can go and clean the wall you've vandalized.'

William's eyes widened. It would take ages.

'Yes,' nodded Mr Salmon grimly, 'even if it takes ages. This vandalism has got to stop. I've told the Head about this, and she agrees with me that we're not prepared to have you going round like a mindless yob, William.'

*

So, once again, while the others went to swimming practice, William was hard at work. He scrubbed away at Tesco's wall. His best friend, Danny Dykins, watched, dangling his legs from the top of one of the bottle banks. He wasn't swimming because of a verruca, so he had been assigned to be William's minder.

William poured some more of the liquid onto his brush. The picture was disappearing gradually, but it was jolly hard work and he was in a fine sweat.

'You ever seen a ghost, Danny?' he asked as he scrubbed away.

'Don't believe in them,' said Danny. 'Why? You seen one?'

'Don't know,' said William slowly.

He described the golden man to Danny, who looked disbelieving.

'Some of these sharp suits they wear now,' he said. 'This Italian gear, designer jackets, you know, they've got a gold thread in them – perhaps he was wearing one of them.'

'Down by the river?'

'Might have been on his way to a disco at the Tiv.'

William wasn't convinced. Besides, the man had been gleaming, dazzling in gold. His mum didn't believe him either.

But by now Tesco's wall was more or less clean. 'Finished,' he said.

He threw the bottle, brush and rags into a carrier.

'I'm whacked,' he said. 'Wish I didn't have to walk all the way back to school.'

'I'll drive you,' offered Danny, jumping down.

'Drive me?'

'Yeah.' He pulled over an abandoned shopping trolley. 'Get in.'

'Hey-hey!' said William, and scrambled into it.

They whizzed across the car park and up the side of the supermarket. William's insides bounced up and down as the trolley clicked over the flagstones. Now the path led up a slope to Chester Street. Danny was beginning to pant. William laughed and slapped the sides of the trolley, 'Gee up, come on there, boy!'

Danny turned the corner so sharply that the trolley could only take the bend on two wheels. The weight of it was just too much for him, and he lost control. The trolley, with William in it, crashed sideways. Danny's feet got caught in the wheels and he fell sprawling on top of the lot.

'Danny Dykins and *William Bellis*!'

Oh, no! William didn't need to look up – it was the Head's voice. He couldn't believe it. Why did things *always* turn sour?

5

They walked home from their appointment with the headteacher.

'I can't believe it,' said Mrs Bellis. 'I just can't believe it – *you* on report. I've never seen Mrs Evans so cross before.'

'She said I'm a quiet, well-behaved pupil normally,' said William. 'You heard her.'

'Yes, but then she went on to say you'd been getting into trouble several times recently. She called you a vandal. *My* son – a *vandal*!'

Words failed her.

William mooched along beside her, hands in his pockets. He was just grateful that Mrs Evans hadn't told his mother any details – about the penknife, for instance.

'So you've got to show me your report card every evening and I've got to sign it.'

'Yup.'

'William – this is serious!'

He scowled.

'I've just had a run of bad luck, that's all.'

'And the first thing you can do when we get home, young man, is to tidy your room. It's an absolute tip. No one wants to see bike parts and oily rags in bedrooms.'

'Who cares about oily rags when the world's in such a mess.'

'William! They will when I show them round.'

'Show them round! Who?'

'Prospective buyers. You know we talked about moving – well, I've put the house up for sale. The estate agents will stick a sign outside tomorrow.'

William felt uneasy. The thought of moving to a new house was fun, but he didn't like the thought of selling his own house. He had always lived there. He certainly didn't fancy strangers looking into his bedroom. Even his mother thought twice about going in there. He asked, 'What about the house we're going to buy?'

'I picked up lots of leaflets at the estate agents. You can look at them later.'

'Now?'

'*No*. When you've tidied your room.'

An hour later Mum came upstairs to inspect. She glanced at the ceiling and sighed.

'You still haven't taken down those tyres.'

'I've got to hang them somewhere, they're my spares.'

'Well, put them somewhere where they can't be seen – how about here, under your bed? Oh, William, what's in this jar? Something's moving.'

'Don't upset them. They're my snails.'

'Snails?'

'Yes, we're training them, Danny and me. He's got some too. We're going to race them. On Sports Day.'

'Well, would you mind keeping them outside, please. And why are all these dirty socks on the windowsill?'

'They're just airing a bit, so I can wear them again.'

'*William*! Put that comic down and sort out this pig-sty. Otherwise there's no supper.'

By eight-thirty he had shifted things about enough for her. She nodded, resigned. 'That'll do.'

'Great, I'm starving.'

William went down the stairs two at a time. He made himself a pickle and banana sandwich and went into the living room.

'A plate, William – you're dropping crumbs – get a plate.'

He fetched a plate and sat down beside his mum, munching. She passed him some of the house advertisements, then looked over his shoulder and commented on each one.

'That's got no garden.

'That's lovely, but it's much too expensive.

'Cheap, but only one bedroom.

'That one's cheap, but it needs a lot doing to it.'

William peered at the picture. Suddenly he realized.

'I know where that is. It's Hen Tŷ, the Old House between the Chester road and the river.'

'It's a good solid stone house, but it's been empty for ages.'

'Aw, great – I'd like to live near the river, so would Jet, and it's near the rugby field too. We could –'

He stopped. He suddenly remembered the Golden Man.

'Yes?' said his mother. She looked up from the leaflet she was reading again.

'Well,' said William, 'I suppose it might be a bit … er … lonely, or … spooky.'

'Nonsense,' she replied. 'There's lots of houses along the road nearby.'

'But it was just there I saw that … golden man.'

'Did Jet bark at him?'

'No, I don't think she saw him … it …'

She was reassuring. 'Like I said, it was probably just a trick of the light. We'd have heard if there was any gossip about the place being haunted or anything …'

It was obvious she didn't believe him. William decided to say nothing more about it for the moment. But his mother was still going on about the Old House.

'Considering how well built it is, it's quite a snip;

though I must say, I'd prefer a nice up-to-date little house myself, with all mod. cons … But I suppose we could just go and look at it at the weekend. And meanwhile, young man, try and keep out of trouble at school. Now: bed.'

Next day at school it was as though nothing had happened. Mrs Evans came out of her room just as William was passing.

'Good morning, William,' she said, and even smiled – no mention of the rather strained interview of the previous day. Old Fishy, too, was his usual self. If anything, he was more considerate than usual, making quite sure William understood the decimals they were working out, and commenting favourably on his designs for a space station.

After playtime it was discussion time. They were to plan their term's project. Mr Salmon leant on the edge of his table and folded his arms. He was wearing a particularly colourful pullover. The girls nearest to him giggled, shading their eyes. He waited patiently.

Planning the term's project was always fun. Last year they'd worked on a garden for the school and, when it was all dug and planted, a real artist had come into school and helped them to make a sculpture for the new garden. It was standing there now among the young trees.

'Our fame seems to have spread,' said Mr Salmon. 'This term we've been asked to work on a large, important project for someone else.'

There was an attentive silence.

'Tesco's supermarket,' he said.

William's heart sank. He never wanted to hear the name Tesco again.

'The management of Tesco's have asked if we would be interested in planning, designing, and planting a large mural for them.'

'What's a mural, sir?'

'A painting on a wall, Danny.'

'A painting on Tesco's wall, sir?'

That was Lindy Lassiter. Word had spread. Heads turned. Faces grinned at William and he was nudged in the ribs. With an expressionless face, Mr Salmon went on:

'Behind the bottle banks there's a long, flat stretch of … er … cleaned … wall, which they say would do very nicely for a mural. They want us to submit a design. If they approve, they'll pay for the materials for us to go ahead.'

William felt a sudden burst of eagerness to work on this.

'What would go on the design, sir?'

'That's for you all to decide.'

'A pattern?' asked Lindy Lassiter.

'Bor-*ing*!'

Lindy blushed.

'A picture from the *Jungle Book*, or *Star Wars*, or something …'

'That's been done hundreds of times.'

'That's just copying, isn't it, sir?'

'Yes,' said Mr Salmon. 'It needs to be original.'

'We could have something about Wales –'

'Or Mold –'

'All the important places in Mold –'

'Yeah – the Red Lion, the Boar's Head, the Leeswood Arms, the Dolphin …'

'Ha, ha,' jeered the others. 'Very good, Jonesey, very witty.'

'That's quite a good idea to pursue,' said Mr Salmon. 'No, not yours, Jonesey – I mean something about Mold.'

'Historical bits?'

'Pictures of what the town's like today?'

'Our ideas for Mold after 2000?'

'Yes, all of that. Why not? We'll have to do some research. Then we'll start work on sketches for it after the weekend.'

Turning to William and Danny he added dryly, 'You never know, this *could* get us back into Tesco's good books.'

6

It was Saturday morning. William's mother was rattling out orders.

'Hurry up, William! It's too late to finish that wiping up – they'll be here any minute. Put that dirty saucepan in the oven for now. Hide Jet's bowl in the cupboard under the sink – quick, look sharp.'

William was amazed. He'd never seen his mother so frenetic. He looked out of the front window yet again.

'There's a car coming round the corner,' he said.

'Oh, help, that must be them – stuff my knitting under

that cushion … Oh, lor', I forgot to clean the windows – the sun shows up every speck, they're filthy. Too late now. Quick, get the air freshener, spray some pine forest about. Put some soothing mood music on – no, *not* Christmas carols, William!'

His mother flung her slippers into the cupboard under the stairs and tottered into her high heels. She peered in the hall mirror, licked her finger and smoothed her eyebrows.

'How do I look?' she asked anxiously.

'*Mum* – they've come to see the house, not you.'

'I know, I know, but we want to give a good first impression, don't we? Where's the dog?'

'On her blanket in the shed. I've shut her in, just for now. She won't bother us.'

The doorbell rang. Mrs Bellis let in a tall man and a woman in a green coat. They stood in the hall and glanced round.

'Mmm, smaller than it looks from outside,' said the woman in a carrying whisper.

William's mother led the way into the kitchen.

'It's quite a good size,' she said timidly.

'Where do you keep your dishwasher?' demanded the woman.

'That's me,' said William chirpily. His mother frowned at him. They trooped into the living room. Everybody looked round. At the same moment they all noticed the cobweb hanging from the light. William wanted to giggle. The woman's glance scoured the walls.

'Magnolia, is it? Of course we'd redecorate immediately.'

They proceeded up the stairs in silence. At the top, the woman pulled up the collar of her coat.

'Have you a window open? There's quite a draught coming from somewhere … Oh, you haven't any double-glazing? Well, that would explain it.'

They entered William's bedroom. He lingered on the stairs listening to the comments. His mother was doing her best.

'This is quite a sizeable room actually – though of course it's difficult to appreciate that when it's full of things.'

'Yes, well, I suppose every house has to have some sort of a junk room …'

The tall man's head bumped against a bicycle wheel, which moved away and swung back against him. He stepped sharply backwards. His companion moved sideways to avoid him. There was a squelching crunch.

'Ugh,' she exclaimed. 'What on earth was that?'

'One of my racing snails,' cried William. 'You've killed it.'

He strode in, glowering at the woman, and dropped to his knees to look under the bed.

'I told you to take them outside!' hissed his mother.

The man, still rubbing his forehead, spoke for the first time. He sounded bemused.

'I think we've seen enough. Come on, Glo.'

Glo was wiping her shoe clean on William's bedside rug with a look of extreme distaste.

'Yes,' she said. 'We'll let you know …'

The front door slammed. William looked at his mother. Her lips were trembling.

'Oh, oh,' she said. 'Oh …'

They caught one another's eye and collapsed in laughter on William's bed.

'Oh dear,' said Mrs Bellis eventually. 'You have to laugh, I suppose …'

She felt in her pocket for a hanky to mop up her tears.

'Oh, look,' she said. 'Here's a letter from Grandfather that came this morning. I've not had a chance to read it yet.'

She sat on the edge of the bed and tore it open. She read it through and said, 'Ah – isn't that nice? The warden of the flats, and the others, are going to celebrate his birthday in style. He'll be ninety in a fortnight, you know. They're going to have a party for him, and he wants us to go.'

'Us? Go down to London?'

William had never been to London.

'We can't, of course – it'd cost too much. And anyway, I can't really leave the house empty at this point – there might be more buyers …'

She laughed again, though more ruefully this time.

'When is it?' William squinted at the letter. 'Look – it's going to be in my half-term.'

'Yes, but I've still got to go to work.'

William nodded. And he was growing really keen on the mural too; he wanted to spend some of half-term making sketches for it. He was suddenly reminded of Old Fishy.

'Mum – what do you think Mold is famous for?'

She considered.

'Well, for a lot of tourists, it's just somewhere on the

way to the seaside, isn't it? But St Mary's is a landmark, and the theatre, and Bethesda Chapel. Then there's the Alleluia Monument, and the Mold torc is supposed to be famous …'

'What's a torc?'

'Search me. Sort of necklace, isn't it? I'm sure I've heard Grandfather mention it. Something to do with Mold, I'm sure. You could write and ask Grandfather.'

Her eyes suddenly lit up.

'I know! *You* could go to Grandfather's party! You could represent us!'

'Me? To London? By myself?'

'Yes, of course. You're in double figures now, and fairly sensible. I'll phone the warden and see if someone could meet you off the coach at Victoria. Grandfather would love to see you, and you could ask him all the questions you wanted.'

William felt excited.

'But what about the fare?'

'Oh, bother the fare. I'll find that. I'll book a seat on the coach for you, then you'll just have to sit tight. How about that?'

William didn't answer. His stomach was already turning over nervously at the idea, but his eyes shone. What an adventure!

His mother turned the letter over.

'Oh, look,' she said, 'he's written a PS specially for you: "*Hope William likes the present. He ought to, he's a sharp lad, a cut above the others …*" What on earth does he mean?'

7

William and his mother went to view several houses in the course of the next few days. But they always seemed to find something wrong – a poky kitchen, no central heating, too small, too high a price.

'Not enough room to swing a cat – or Jet,' said Mrs Bellis, more than once.

'We'll have to stay here,' said William one evening, half-pleased, half-disappointed.

'We really can't afford to any longer,' said his mum. She sighed and ran her fingers through her curly hair. She looked again at the sheaf of advertisements in her hands.

'I suppose we still haven't been to look at the Old House behind Pentre. It sounds almost derelict, but it's cheap. The owner lives abroad and wants to get rid of it.'

An image of the Golden Man flashed into William's mind. He was *sure* it hadn't been the reflection of the setting sun …

On Monday evening they set out together for the Chester road. They passed the rugby field. Then they turned off it and went along a little path between the sides of the houses and their gardens. This was the only access to the Old House.

'Suppose we had a car?' said William. 'We wouldn't be able to drive it to the house.'

His mother looked vague.

'I suppose that's why no one's been interested in buying the place,' she answered.

The estate agent hadn't bothered to come with them. He'd handed them the key and glanced at their feet.

'You'll need your wellies when you go there,' he said briefly.

The Old House lay half hidden, tucked into the hillside behind the road. It was an old Welsh longhouse. Long and low, built of stone, it looked as though it hadn't been touched for decades, ignored and forgotten by the twentieth century. Nettles and ragwort surrounded its grimy, whitewashed walls.

William and his mother waded through the waist-high weeds.

'Someone grew raspberries here once,' she said, holding back some overgrown canes.They reached the faded blue front door. Cut into the long stone above the door were the letters S.B. The whitewash on the walls was flaking, slightly patched with green where algae was growing.

Mrs Bellis took hold of the handle and pushed her thumb down. The latch rattled and gave way.

'I didn't need the key,' she said. 'It opened easily.'

They went from room to room. They were grey with dust and cobwebs. Bird droppings and bits of nests were scattered in the large fireplaces and over the floor near the hearths.

'There's only a fire to cook on in the kitchen,' said Wiiliam's mother. 'It's all so primitive.'

'Here's the scullery,' said William. 'There's a stone sink, and a water tap. Look, Mum, water comes out of the tap!'

'Big deal,' said his mother. 'Oh, William, there's no way we could live here.'

William guided her to the three windows in the main room.

'Look,' he said. 'Just down there.'

About ten metres down the grassy slope ran the Alyn. It was so quiet in the room, that they could hear the water trickling. A wagtail ran along the edge of the pebbles.

'It's very peaceful,' admitted William's mother, 'but think of the work to get this place habitable.'

'*I* could do some,' said William eagerly, 'and Danny Dykins would help, and some of the others in my class.'

William's mum laughed ruefully.

'And there's no electricity, no gas, no telephone –'

'No nothing really,' said William cheerfully. 'But they'd soon bring electricity over from the Chester road, and at least there's water already. Oh, Mum – go on, say we can live here, it's great.'

'William, you're such a baby! It would be almost impossible to buy this place. What about drains, for instance?'

'*Drains*?'

'Yes, dear, drains. It's nearly the year 2000. You can't live without drains any more.'

'Oh, *Mum* …'

They spent another half hour there, exploring the rooms and imagining how they could arrange them.

'There's masses of room in the shippen for my bike and stuff,' said William enthusiastically. He was completely convinced this was the place for them. His mother was less certain.

Back in the office the estate agent held out his hand for the key.

'No good?' he asked, not expecting an answer.

'We-ell …' said Mrs Bellis. She laughed.

The agent spun round, raising his eyebrows. William's mum laughed again. 'I'd be interested if the price was brought down … er … £10,000 …'

Now it was the agent's turn to laugh, in disbelief. But they could see there was a gleam in his eye. He scented a sale.

'Very unlikely,' he said. 'But I'll contact the vendor, who lives abroad. I'll be in touch with you as soon as I can.'

They left the office.

'No one's likely to drop £10,000 from the asking price,' said William's mother. 'I was just trying it on really. Besides, I've made an appointment to go and see those modern flats near the church later this week.'

Half-term was approaching. William was growing excited about his visit to London. Meanwhile, in class, they were busy researching the history of Mold. They had brought reference books from the library. They had read about the battle near the town. They had visited St Mary's Church, and Bethesda Chapel, and they had been out sketching some of the town's modern buildings.

The children had plenty of ideas for the mural, but only William had felt sufficiently fired by the project to make detailed designs and hand them in. Mr Salmon seemed impressed. He spread them out on a table.

'These are good, William,' he said. 'I'm sure they can be the basis for the final design.'

'Oh, thanks, sir,' beamed William. 'But don't you think we should put in some people? We've got plenty of ideas for buildings, but we ought to put in some *people*.'

'You're quite right,' said Mr Salmon in surprise. 'Quite right, William. There'd be no history without people. And all these buildings we've been looking at only exist because people thought they were necessary for one reason or another. Unfortunately, the buildings remain, while the people who planned and built them are long dead.'

William reflected on this. Then he said, 'Do you believe in ghosts, sir?'

Mr Salmon considered.

'I don't think I've ever seen one,' he said, 'though I suppose there could be such things. "There are more things in heaven and earth than are dreamt of …"'

Danny blurted out, 'William says he's seen a ghost, sir.'

William glared at his friend, and Mr Salmon looked questioningly at them. The rest of the class was suddenly quiet.

'It was just a man, sir,' said William, 'down near the river. He had long hair, and his shoulders and chest were shining, dazzling gold, like brilliant gold, sir. I was nearly blinded, like when you catch the sun in your eyes. And then he disappeared.'

There was a moment's silence. Then Lindy Lassiter sniggered.

'Shurrup, Lassie!' hissed Danny fiercely.

Mr Salmon took no notice of the interruption. He went on looking seriously at William.

'Perhaps you could draw what you saw, William? That would make you try and remember it in detail. Bring it in after half-term. I'd be interested to see it.'

William and Danny cycled home by way of Tesco's. They took another look at the wall.

'It's awfully long,' said Danny. 'We'll never manage to fill that, even if we all have a go at painting.'

'Yes, we will,' said William confidently.

'It'll take pots and pots of paint,' said Danny.

'Buckets,' said William, 'barrels.'

'Vats,' agreed Danny. 'Tanker-loads.'

They celebrated the start of the week's holiday by sharing a can of Coke.

'Danny,' said William. 'Do you know what a torc is?'

'A torc?' said Danny. He narrowed his eyes in thought. 'Something they give on the radio?'

'Moron!'

William grinned and shook his head. He would ask Great-grandfather.

Later that evening, when William's mother opened the post, she cried out when she realized that one envelope included a cheque.

'It's from Grandfather for your coach fare. Isn't he an absolute duck?'

8

The day arrived for the London trip. William forbade his mother to accompany him to the coach stop. But her last-minute instructions and messages for Great-grandfather lasted from the moment William got up until she hugged him goodbye. Danny turned up unexpectedly and insisted on cycling alongside him with William's rucksack balanced on the handlebars. William felt quite a pang of nerves as he waved down to him from his window in the coach. His seat, half-way back, gave him a high view over the countryside. Twenty minutes out of Mold, the coach sped past a sign marking the border between Wales and England. Home suddenly seemed much further away. Luckily, William's mother had packed him a huge bag of lunch which he felt duty bound to polish off within the first hour.

He spent a long time watching the other traffic on the motorway, and he had brought a cycling magazine to read. The coach stopped in Birmingham coach station, where there was plenty to look at, so the time passed pleasantly. As they approached London, the motorway grew more and more congested. Then they made their way through dense traffic for several kilometres. William was glad when they eventually drove into Victoria coach station.

He went down the steps of the coach with his rucksack, and stood waiting, as arranged. The air was full of the strong smell of diesel fumes and a noise of engines.

He was quite bewildered by the jostling bustle of other travellers. Great-grandfather had promised he would be met – but by whom? Perhaps Mrs Goodfellow, the warden of the flats?

A large black London taxi drew up alongside him. The door behind the driver opened.

'William?'

'Great-grandfather!'

'Get in, boy, get in – the less time you spend breathing in these noxious fumes, the better.'

William slung his rucksack onto the floor of the cab and clambered in, slamming the door behind him. The interior was as large as a small room. He turned to look at his great-grandfather, and they eyed one another affectionately. They hadn't met for five years, but the old man looked just the same. He was completely bald, though he still had those thick black eyebrows William remembered. He also seemed to be wearing the same brown suit, with a red waistcoat, and a watch in his top pocket attached to a chain which hung across his rounded middle. His dark eyes looked his great-grandson up and down.

'Well, William, it's a good thing your mother said you'd be carrying a green rucksack, I'd hardly have recognized you else. I reckon you've grown two inches for every year since I saw you last.'

William grinned happily. The old man took his watch from his breast pocket and looked at it.

'Well now, it's just before two o'clock. They've told me I'm to keep out of the way until eight, when the party starts. What a lot of fuss! All because the good Lord has let me stay here until I'm ninety. They keep congratulating me – it's none of my doing, I tell them. Silly women!'

He sighed dramatically, but looked pleased at the same time.

The taxi engine was still ticking over. The driver turned and asked sarcastically, 'Stayin' 'ere all day, are we?'

The old man took no notice. He said to William: 'We've got six hours of freedom – what shall we do? Where shall we go? The whole of the metrop lies before us? Eh?'

The driver shrugged and switched on the radio. William's mind was a blank.

'Got it,' said Great-grandfather. 'The Science Museum.'

'Oh, great,' said William, 'there was a programme about it on telly.'

The driver had obviously been listening, for without further ado he put the cab into gear and they glided out of the coach station. Great-grandfather fired questions at William: 'How's your mother? Have you sold the house? Have you found somewhere else to live?'

William's life in Wales seemed thousands of kilometres away.

'Did you like the birthday present?' asked the old man.

'Oh, yes,' William exclaimed. 'But I didn't show it to Mum.'

He described the events which had followed and the old man rocked with laughter.

'So your teacher is called Old Fishy? One of mine was called Walrus. Do you like him?'

'Oh yes, he's OK really. We're painting a mural after

40

half-term. And Mum said I was to ask you about the Mold torc.'

'The Mold torc. My dear boy, we'll arrange that right away.'

He leant forward and tapped on the glass partition behind the driver.

'Change of plan,' he said. 'Make it the British Museum.'

William thought the driver hadn't heard, but the taxi swung round in an amazing U-turn and set off in another direction.

The old man's brown eyes were bright with excitement.

'Our family has connections with the Mold torc, you know. *My* grandfather was there when it was dug up. He was Billy, you know. There's always been a William in the family – I'm Will myself.'

That was news to William.

'Yes, Billy was there when it was dug up. He was only a lad of ten, but he never forgot. He would tell the story if he was prompted. He said he was the first one at the time who picked it up and looked at it closely. And in fact, my great-aunt Sophie –'

He broke off, as the brakes squealed.

'British Museum, squire,' said the driver. 'Fifteen quid.'

'Fifteen quid!' exclaimed the old man. 'Daylight robbery!'

'Well, if you have your family reunions in a taxi, it *will* cost you an arm and a leg, won't it?'

Great-grandfather snorted and pushed two notes at him. They got out. The taxi swung away and William looked round. They were in a vast square courtyard, with high buildings round three sides. In front of them was the main entrance of the British Museum, guarded by enormous pillars. The old man led the way up the steps. William had to open his rucksack to show a uniformed security woman what was inside.

'Why?' he whispered to Great-grandfather.

'They don't want anyone bombing the place,' hissed the old man. 'The stuff in here is absolutely priceless.'

They went into the enormous entrance hall where William left his rucksack in the cloakroom.

'Follow me,' said Great-grandfather.

He stumped up the echoing stone staircase, quite at home. They reached the top, both panting slightly, but Great-grandfather didn't pause – past a Roman mosaic, past the preserved body of a man found in a peat bog, and – 'There!' said Great-grandfather, standing four-square in front of a tall glass case. 'There's our torc. What do you make of *that*?'

William stood and stared. It wasn't at all what he was expecting. In the case was a golden cape, made to fit snugly over someone's shoulders and upper arms. Curving lines of embossed squares, triangles, ovals and circles ran round it, following the shape of a human body from neck down to elbow, like joined layers of necklaces. Running round the lower edge was a line of holes. Here and there the cape had been mended, and there was a small piece missing at the bottom. But the cape's most striking quality was its colour: a soft, shining, glowing gold.

'Wow!' said William. But surely he knew the cape?

Surely he'd seen it already? 'Do you mean that was dug up in Mold?'

Great-grandfather nodded proudly.

'Yes, on the slope between the rugby field and Pentre.' Then he added: 'Though it was buried more than 3000 years ago, long before there was a rugby field or a place called Pentre.'

William went on staring at the torc. His heart was beating fast and a wave of heat pulsed through his body; he felt suddenly dizzy.

The old man went on talking.

'No one knows who it belonged to, or where it was made, or why it was buried there. Nothing like it has been found anywhere else in Europe. It's priceless. It's unique. But –' he turned to William, 'what we *do* know is that my grandfather Billy was there on the October day they dug it up in 1833. And there was talk of giving it to the scrap man!'

William was drawing in deep breaths to steady himself. His gaze was fixed on the golden torc. But his mind's eye was 300 kilometres away, down by the river Alyn in Mold, watching a shimmering mirage, a man, a Golden Man. He suddenly realized, with a shock of absolute certainty, that the man he had seen in the dazzle of the setting sun had been wearing this same golden cape.

'Great-grandfather,' he whispered, 'do you believe in ghosts?'

9

It was quarter to seven when their third taxi of the day eventually drew up outside the block of flats.

'Here we are,' said Great-grandfather. 'Welcome to the Four Aitches.'

They stepped out onto the gravel and William looked round. A garden full of flowers surrounded them, and the cream stone building, three storeys high, rose above them. A notice near the main door identified the flats as 'Happy Homes for the Hale and Hearty'.

'That's me,' said Great-grandfather, pounding his chest so hard that the rose fell out of his button-hole. 'Ninety today and feel like thirty.'

He grinned happily at William. 'It's been a wonderful afternoon, boy – thank you. First the Mold torc; it brought tears to my eyes seeing that again. And then the Science Museum – amazing place. All those machines you can switch on and get working – incredible ingenuity. I don't think I've ever enjoyed a birthday afternoon so much. Apart from all those tiresome youngsters, that is …'

William laughed. In the Science Museum Great-grandfather had made a bee-line for every working model, determined to have a turn, elbowing aside children about a tenth of his age.

The main door of the flats swung open. Three women in smart dresses smiled a welcome.

'Oh, they're in their glad rags already,' muttered Great-grandfather. 'We'd better go and get spruced up

44

ourselves. But first come and meet Dilly, Tilly and Philly.' In the centre of the group stood a big red-faced woman in a red dress. Her hair was piled up in a large round shape, like a cottage loaf, on the top of her head. She beamed at him.

'Mr Will, dear, you're here at last. We were beginning to fear you'd miss your own party.'

'And we've made salmon pinwheels, smoked oyster tartlets, and chocolate strawberries,' piped up a tiny woman with bright blue eyes.

'And there was me thinking you'd be making me leek stew and Welsh goat's cheese pie,' teased Great-grandfather; then added, 'Allow me to introduce my great-grandson, William.'

The ladies gathered round.

'All the way from Wales!' said the third woman, dressed in black silk. William eyed her pearl ear-rings and necklace.

'William, this is Mrs Goodfellow – known as Miss Dilly. This is Miss Tilly, and Miss Philly – the three Graces.'

'Oh, Mr Will!'

They laughed and fluttered, and shook William's hand in turn.

'What a long way to come,' said Miss Philly, fingering her pearl necklace.

'But for such a special occasion!' said Miss Tilly. 'We've got a marvellous spread ready.'

'Mr Will is one of our most popular residents,' said Miss Dilly to William, her red face flushing even redder with pleasure.

'Now, now, Miss Dilly,' said Great-grandfather. 'Less of your flattery, don't forget the time I fused all the lights –'

'And broke a chair, sitting down too hard –'

'And kept everybody awake with your singing, when Wales trounced England at Twickenham.'

'You see?' said Great-grandfather to William, 'I'm the villain of the flats really. Now, ladies, I'm going to take William upstairs for a quick wash and brush-up.'

'We'll see you in the common room at eight then,' smiled little Miss Tilly.

Great-grandfather led the way through the hall to the lift. There was just space for William, with his rucksack on his back, to squeeze in with him. They got out on the third floor.

'It's just by here,' said Great-grandfather, stopping outside door number 33.

'*Fy nhy*,' he announced, '"my house". Do you speak Welsh at all, boy?'

'A little,' said William. '*Tipyn bach*. We learn it at school.'

Great-grandfather nodded sadly.

'I don't speak it much now,' he said. 'I don't get the chance, though we spoke only Welsh at home, of course, and in the quarry. Then when I joined the railway it had to be all English.'

He fished in his pocket for a key.

'Mum goes to Welsh classes,' said William.

'And her from Devon – there's nice,' said Great-grandfather. 'She's a good girl, your mother. Young Gwilym was a fool to walk out and leave you both.'

William flushed. He mumbled something about him and his mother managing OK.

'Of course you do, boy. I know you do. It's just that there's times when a boy needs a father as well as a mother.'

The old man sighed and unlocked the door.

'Come on in now, and make yourself at home. Kitchen's there, lavatory's by there in the bathroom. I'll just make a quick cuppa before we go down for the official binge. I'd rather have a good cup of tea than champers any day.'

William looked round the large room. There was a bed against one wall, two easy chairs and a settee, a table, television set, a wardrobe, a bookcase, a striped rug on the floor, yellow curtains, a view over a big garden and a tree near the window where a thrush was singing. It felt comfortable.

On the bookcase stood a worn old bronze candlestick surrounded by birthday cards. Hanging on the walls were pictures of one or two places William recognized from home – the Clwydian hills at sunset, Moel Fammau mountain, St Mary's Church. His attention was drawn to a large brownish photograph in a carved frame. An old man with a walrus moustache was sitting very upright with one hand on the arm of a sofa. He held his other hand pressed to his waistcoat and watch-chain, as he stared straight at the camera in a dignified manner.

Next to him on the settee sat a white-haired old lady in a high-collared blouse with long sleeves. She was looking down with a half-smile at a serious baby in a white dress and little black button boots, who was sitting on her lap.

'Who is it?' asked William, going close to look at it.

'The old man was my grandfather Billy, and the old lady was my grandmother. Liesel she was called; she was Swiss. It was taken in a portrait studio in Mold in 1907, when I was just a year old.'

'*You*? That's you with them?'

'Yes, boy. You can't believe I was a baby once?'

William stared at the photo. The old man went on.

'They must be your – let's see – your great-great-great-grandparents. I remember them well. They died when I was about ten. They were very proud of their age. They used to say, "We've been Georgian, Victorian, Edwardian, and now we're Georgian again." They both lived into their nineties – same as I hope to – if I survive the party tonight!'

He laughed. Then he gestured towards the photograph.

'You see the old man's watch-chain?'

William looked at the portrait and nodded. The chain curved over the old man's front from one pocket to another.

'Well,' said Great-grandfather. 'Here it is.'

William turned. He looked closely at Great-grandfather's watch-chain for the first time. It, too, swung across his stomach from one small pocket to another larger one, where he kept his heavy silver watch. William remembered sitting on Great-grandfather's knee many times when he was little, half entranced as the watch was held swinging and ticking in front of him.

'Yes, this was that very chain,' said Great-grandfather. He left it to my father, and my father left it to me – and I shall be leaving it to you, boy.'

It was a solid silver chain with something hanging from it – a pendant, a thick yellowy-orange ring, the same size as a peppermint with a hole in it, but polished smooth as glass. Great-grandfather pointed at the photo.

'You can just make it out, look, by there. He was very attached to it, was grandfather Billy, though I'm not quite sure why. Perhaps because his sister Sophie had it made into an ornament for his watch chain when he was twenty-one. Amber it is, an amber bead cut in half, then polished. Nice, eh?'

William ran his finger over the smooth surface of the tawny disc. Great-grandfather looked at the photograph for a long moment, then he recalled himself to the present and made for the kitchen.

'Now, what's your preference, boy,' he called over his shoulder. 'Assam? Darjeeling? Earl Grey? Or common old tea bag?'

10

Right, boy – it's a minute to eight. Ready?'

William nodded. He had washed and changed into the clean jeans and white polo-necked shirt his mother had insisted he brought. He put his hand on his stomach.

'I feel a bit nervous,' he confided.

Great-grandfather laughed.

'You'll be OK. They're all nice people. Right, let's go – into the valley of death. We won't use the lift, we'll go down the stairs, and make the entry that becomes a nonagenarian on his birthday.'

The common room was already full, and there was a little outburst of applause as Great-grandfather entered. William recognized the lady in black, Miss Philly, who came over to him.

'William, come and have a glass of something. What would you like? There's orange juice, red or white wine, Coke, sherry, champagne, cider?'

William remembered what Great-grandfather had said about champagne and asked for cider. Great-grandfather himself had obviously forgotten, and was moving round the room chatting and holding a glass of champagne in each hand. He seemed to be enjoying himself hugely after all.

Several people came to talk to William. Lots of them seemed to have stayed in Rhyl or Llandudno, or had been to Chester at some time. It was nice to talk about places he knew. He began to feel less nervous – and the bubbly golden cider was delicious.

At last Miss Dilly rose to her feet and clinked a spoon against a cup for silence.

'Ladies and gentlemen,' she said, 'on the occasion of his ninetieth birthday, we are privileged to be able to tell Mr Will Bellis how much we appreciate him [cheers], and how interesting he makes life for the rest of us residents here ["Yes, true."].'

She turned to Great-grandfather.

'Mr Will, we considered carefully what sort of little gift would give you most pleasure, and many people mentioned your love of our beautiful garden here. So our present to you is outside in the garden itself. And as it's such a pleasant evening, let's go and see it.'

She made for the main door, followed by the residents. Some walked with a stick, one or two leaned on zimmer frames, but chatting cheerfully, they all made their way out through the front door. When they were assembled on the gravel, Miss Dilly pointed dramatically to her left.

'*Voilà*!' she announced.

They all turned. Next to a small tree stood a wooden garden bench.

'Hey, that's nice,' said Great-grandfather admiringly.

'Yes, Mr Will, for you – a William pear tree, and a comfortable bench. You can sit on one and watch the other one grow.'

Everyone smiled. Great-grandfather bent to look at the brass plate. He read the inscription aloud:

> '*Presented to Mr William Bellis*
> *on the occasion of his ninetieth birthday.*'

'Well,' he said, struggling for words for once. 'Well …'

The other residents clapped and crowded round to shake hands with Great-grandfather as he tried to thank them. Then he was photographed sitting on the bench, first alone, then with William next to him. One of the other old men, Mr Cyril, plump and fluffy-haired, said cleverly, 'A William pear and a pair of Williams,' and everyone laughed.

Then they trooped inside and made for the buffet.

William was feeling rather peculiar by now, and suddenly realized that he was famished. His eyes widened at the spread – sausages on sticks, dips of all sorts, crisps and nibbles, cheeses, pies, salads, striped pinwheels, savoury tartlets, chocolate strawberries, meringues, trifle, lemon cheesecake, fruit salad and cream slices.

The residents obviously relished their food, and once or twice William found himself being edged out of his place in the queue. He grinned to himself.

'Enjoying yourself, boy?' asked Great-grandfather, standing at his side with a plate piled high.

'Yes, it's great,' answered William, 'and I've just remembered something I had to –'

'Whoops,' interrupted Great-grandfather. 'They want me to cut the cake.'

He made his way over to a table which had been placed in the centre of the room. On it was a large cake in the shape of a figure ninety, iced in red and white.

'The team colours of the London Welsh, Will,' pointed out Mr Cyril.

'And nine candles, one for each decade,' said Great-grandfather.

He drew in deeply and blew out the nine candles in one breath. To the applause of the guests, he cut the cake into a score of slices. Other residents bustled around with plates of cake.

'Three cheers for old Will,' called Mr Cyril. 'Hip, hip – hurray.'

They raised their glasses and drank. Great-grandfather, suddenly tired, looked round and waved his thanks to everyone.

'We've had a wonderful evening, thank you all so much. But now I think it's time I got young William here to bo-bo's.'

William blushed deeply, as Great-grandfather took his arm and led him off to the lift.

'Sorry about that, boy, but enough is enough. Besides, you're off home tomorrow, and I wanted a bit longer to talk to you. What was it you were going to say when I interrupted?'

They were entering room 33 again.

'I was going to say that I'd forgotten to give you your present, Great-grandfather,' said William, 'from Mum and me.'

He went over to his rucksack and brought out two parcels. Great-grandfather opened them eagerly.

'A bottle of Scotch whisky – well, I shall enjoy that. Your mother remembers what I like. And this, what's this? – oh, a framed photo of your mother and yourself – how nice. I shall drink a nip of whisky every night as a night-cap toast to you both.'

Simultaneously they felt the urge to pull off their shoes, and then both flopped onto the settee.

'Ah, that's good,' breathed Great-grandfather, shutting his eyes.

'There was something you were going to tell me in the taxi,' said William, 'something about your Great-aunt Sophie.'

'What were we talking about at the time?'

'The Mold torc. And you said, "In fact, my Great-aunt Sophie …" but you didn't finish.'

'Ah, yes, I remember now. Well, in fact, my Great-aunt

Sophie was quite a character I believe, though she died when she was only in her forties. Grandfather Billy was very fond of her, she was his only sister, and when he found the torc … well, somehow – he was always vague about this – somehow a bit of it remained in his possession. But anyway, he kept it and eventually had it made into a little ring for her. He told me she had exceptionally beautiful white hands, and she always wore this gold ring, in a sort of plaited pattern, on her middle finger, until she lost it doing gardening, which she loved.'

'Like you.'

'Yes, like me. But instead of growing portly and ancient like me, she grew pale and thin, poor thing. Grandmother Liesel was very good to her – gave her money when her father and brother Meic were killed in the pit disaster. Then Sophie and her mother moved away from home and rented a house to run a little school, but one of her pupils had consumption, you see, and poor Sophie caught it from her and just wasted away.'

'Where was the school?'

'In Mold. It was an old house she rented, nearly derelict, so she got it for a peppercorn rent from the landlord. He was a Mr Langford – Grandfather Billy's boss, in fact. The house was derelict again the last time I saw it. We boys used to play near it down by the river.'

'Down by the river?' echoed William.

'Yes,' said Great-grandfather. 'Near where you said you saw your golden ghost.'

'Mum and I went to look at a house down there,' said William excitedly.

'Well, there you are then,' said Great-grandfather

comfortably. 'Your Great-great-aunt Sophie would approve, I'm sure.'

By teatime next day William was home.

'I want to hear *all* about everything you did,' said his mother as she prepared their meal, 'from the moment you stepped off the coach.'

As William unpacked his rucksack, he told her about Great-grandfather and the taxis, the visit to the British Museum and the Science Museum, and then the evening in the Four Aitches.

'Oh, and he's sent you this bronze candlestick. It's a bit battered, he says, but it's been in the family a long time.'

He stopped for breath and a long drink of tea. Jet pressed up close to his knees, making up for his two-day absence.

'There's just one tiny bit of news from this end,' said his mother, pouring her own tea. 'The estate agent rang to say that my ridiculously low offer for the Old House has been agreed! He got in touch with the vendor, a Miss Langford, who lives in Jersey, and she's accepted it.'

'Oh, brill,' said William through a mouthful of buttered crumpet. 'Do you know, Mum, that Great-grandfather's Great-aunt Sophie used to live in the Old House. Isn't that amazing?'

'Goodness, I had no idea,' said his mother. 'How incredible.'

'But I wish I knew more about her, and the way Great-grandfather's grandfather Billy found the torc and everything.'

'I thought you were going to ask Great-grandfather all about it.'

'Yes, but there wasn't that much time, and anyway I think he told me most of what he remembered. But I want to know more. I need to know for the mural. We start painting it next week. I *wish* I could find out more about Great-grandfather's grandfather Billy when he was young.'

Mold, North Wales

1833

1

The river and the water meadows glowed in the golden September sunlight. Billy sat down on the springy turf at the edge of the Alyn. The grass was warm beneath him. He bent over and undid his bootlaces with inky fingers, then eased off the boots with great care. He winced as they rubbed over raw skin. His brother Meic had already worn them for several months, and they were moulded to the shape of his feet. No wonder they hurt Billy.

But it was lucky, really, thought Billy, that he was big for his age, and had the same size feet as his older brother – well, very nearly the same size – so that boots could always be passed on to him to wear out.

Billy lowered his tingling toes into the water, then pushed his cap back on his head. He shut his eyes and let the sunshine warm his face as the cool water rippled round his liberated feet.

There was a sudden rattle of pebbles, a flurry of splashing, eager panting. Without opening his eyes, Billy said, 'Don't disturb me Rats, just seek, go on – seek.'

The black and white terrier leapt away and thrashed through the shallows, nosing into holes in the bank.

Billy lay back, perfectly content. His thoughts turned back to that day's school. He pictured Miss Griffiths's elegant millinery shop on the High Street, and the poky little schoolroom in the back parlour with its benches and desks that were now much too tight for him. How he hated the squeak of the slate pencil on those slates! And even though he was old enough to be allowed to use pen and ink to practise his copperplate cup-hooks, he still wasn't much of a hand at writing – and never would be, however much he was punished.

He opened his eyes and looked at the three red lines across his palm. Only three today. He heard Miss Griffiths's shrill voice again.

'Since I see from my register, William Bellis, that you are ten years of age today, and have decided to leave at midday, I shall be lenient. I shall give you only three strokes of the cane to remember us by.'

He sat up and lowered his hand into the water to cool it. Rats took this as a sign that Billy wanted to play throwing stones, and barked eagerly. One black ear stood on end, the other was neatly folded down like the corner of a page. Billy threw a pebble along the stream. Rats leapt away again between walls of spray.

Billy pulled his hand, dripping, from the water. It still looked red and swollen, though it felt cooler. He pictured Miss Griffiths – brown hair wound round her head under her lace cap, brown dress, brown button boots, brown button eyes, even brownish patches on the backs of her hands. He knew those fat little hands off by heart – stacking the pupils' weekly pennies in piles of twelve, pointing scornfully at the blots on his copybook, or clenched round the end of her cane. He could see her now, narrowing her eyes and pressing her lips together as she brought down the cane with a thwack.

Never no more, though, thought Billy with great satisfaction. *I'm ten today, and I'm nearly a man – Mam had said so this morning – and I'm danged if I need to go back there again just to be beat.*

He threw another stone for Rats and smiled to himself.

I've left now for good. I'll find some work. Mam can do with the money; no need for her to struggle any more to find my pennies for Miss Griffiths neither.

Perhaps he'd even earn enough one day to buy a new pair of boots – just for him! And perhaps something nice for little Jen-next-door; something she'd really like, a toy or a barley sugar stick. And perhaps some lace or a brooch for Sophie. Billy looked again at his wet palm and imagined it full of shillings and florins – or even gold sovereigns.

He knotted the bootlaces together and hung the boots round his neck. Then he pulled himself to his feet.

'Rats – here, boy!'

He whistled and the dog came racing back and danced round him. They made their way along the bank. On the other side of the Alyn, cows were browsing in the water meadows; on this side, Mold village side, the bank sloped quickly upwards for several hundred yards of fallow grassland. This stretch was known as Cae Ellyllon – the field of the elves. 'A pretty name for a pretty place,' Mold people always said, then changed the subject.

Billy's bare feet padded through the long grass. He pushed through the last of the summer's yellow ragwort and then began to climb uphill away from the Alyn stream. Halfway up the Ellyllon field stood the Old

House – Hen Tŷ – tucked into the slope.

The low stone building was gradually being claimed back by the earth, for a tall army of stinging nettles guarded the doors and windows from trespassers, while ivy was already clawing at much of the solid slate roof.

Rats nosed his way into a thicket of tall pink willow herb and disappeared. Billy stood and considered Hen Tŷ. It was low, but it was long; there was probably much more room in there than in the little cottage the five of them lived in on Milford Street. His mam sometimes looked round their cluttered little kitchen and said:

'We haven't even room to swing a mouse …'

But, thought Billy, if the weeds and nettles round Hen Tŷ were scythed down and cleared away … if a pump was put in for water – that shouldn't be difficult, it was only a hundred yards from the Alyn – if the ivy tangles were pulled down, and the slates cleaned … the walls whitewashed … the door painted a fresh green, or blue …

Billy saw it all – he couldn't wait to get home and suggest it to Meic. His brother, Meic, was hoping to marry his sweetheart, Beti, as soon as they found somewhere to live.

Suddenly Rats shot out from the thicket. He raced towards Billy and leapt at him, making him stagger on the tussocky ground.

'Down, boy!' said Billy, fending the dog off.

Rats whined and pressed against Billy's legs.

'What was it? A rat? Step on a thistle?'

Billy slapped the dog's side to encourage him.

'C'mon, let's go.'

They set off to the top of the bank, Billy striding out,

and Rats staying close, whining quietly to himself. At the top of the slope lay the road which ran from the Welsh village of Mold to Chester, in England. Billy often watched as horses pulled creaking coaches along the rutted track, churning up mud and lurching into pot-holes. He longed to stand with other travellers by the pillars of the Black Lion in the High Street, waiting to clamber aboard the 'Wonder' on its way to Barmouth or far-away Liverpool. He had never been to England, but he intended to, as soon as he had some money of his own. (There it was again – was nothing possible without money?)

He reached the top of the meadow. A gang of local men were labouring by the side of the Chester road. William wanted to get a good view of what they were doing, so he climbed up onto the Ellyllon hillock at the top of the field. He sat down with Rats at his side, and watched them.

He recognized most of the men, poor and elderly, often on parish relief. This must be yet more emergency work on the surface of the Chester road; Mold people said the pot-holes opened up overnight, like mushrooms in reverse.

The men had cut a kind of small quarry into the high side of the road, and were shovelling out gravel which they were then loading into a cart. A little bay mare stood patiently between the shafts. Her harness clanked as she browsed in the long grass under the hedge.

The men were working under the supervision of a man on horseback, who was pointing with a whip, giving some sort of instructions. Billy knew him well; it was Mr Langford of Pentre farm. In school holidays Billy sometimes worked for him, digging potatoes, collecting stones, walking the sown fields with the clappers as bird scarer, or helping the cowherd with the pedigree heifers.

'He'll give me work,' Billy murmured to Rats. 'I'm ten and strong. I can dig, same as them over there. I'll go and talk to him now.'

Billy undid the laces and carefully pulled on the boots over his blistered feet. He did them up as fast as he could, then fished a bit of string from his pocket and tied it to the dog's collar. Walking as smartly as he could, though in some pain, he approached Mr Langford.

The men kept their heads down, digging and loading. The gravel landed in the cart with a hiss and a rattle. The farmer looked down at Billy and Rats. The boy's clothes were too big for him, and his boots were poor, but there was an eager expression on his pale face. Mr Langford knew the boy was a good worker.

'Billy?' he nodded in greeting.

'Good afternoon, sir.'

Billy spoke the English carefully, wanting to make a good impression. He pulled off his cap and held it tightly between his hands. He was suddenly nervous. His heart was thumping. This was so important. What should he say? He blurted out in Welsh, 'I'm ten today, sir, left school midday. You got any work?'

2

Billy couldn't wait to get home. He felt a different person altogether from the boy with the pocket full of bread and cheese, who had reluctantly dragged his feet uphill to school this morning. Just wait till he told them his news!

His mood was infectious. Rats had stopped whining and was leaping excitedly round him as he hobbled as fast as he could down the hill from Pentre towards Mold. Once out of sight of Mr Langford and the gang of labourers, Billy sat on the edge of a ditch and eased off his boots again. He was distracted for a moment by a frog hopping through the grass. He picked it up and put it deep in his pocket. Then he slung the boots round his neck and set off at a run. He raced up the slope over Pont Erwyl and up the Chester road to the Cross.

'Hi, Billy!'

He slewed to a halt in the dirt and looked round. His friend Pawl was leaning wearily on the edge of the horse trough, wearing his blue and white striped butcher's apron. His delivery basket, covered with a white cloth, was resting at his feet. Rats heard a voice he recognized and scented the contents of the basket. He trotted over to Pawl who kicked out at him good-humouredly.

'Call him off, Billy. Vicar'll skin me alive if anything happens to this beef.'

'Rats – here boy!' called Billy, then burst out: 'Guess

what – I'm starting work tomorrow.'

'Who with?'

'Old Langford at Pentre farm.'

Pawl looked at Billy admiringly.

'Good for you. He'll work you hard, but there's always extras on farms – you'll see – couple of turnips, a few potatoes, bit of cheese.'

Billy said: 'I get tuppence a week to start, and half a stone of potatoes.'

'See what I mean?' said Pawl. He fended Rats off again, this time with more force. The terrier yelped.

'Come on, Rats,' said Billy, 'we'll go and tell them at home.'

'I'll walk as far as the vicarage with you,' said Pawl, lifting up the delivery basket with an effort. 'Vicar must have company – never seen such a great piece of sirloin before.'

They walked together up the High Street. The boys knew one another from their few years in Miss Griffiths's dame school and had often shared a caning for some misdeed or other. They chatted as they walked. Pawl shifted the basket from arm to arm. Rats made occasional detours to sniff in the gutter or in shop door-ways. The top of the slope was overshadowed by the pale sandstone tower of St Mary's Church, but a few doors down from Church Lane they realized they were passing Miss Griffiths's 'Modish Millinery'. Billy's heart sank, until he remembered that he had left school – for ever! He put his hand on his friend's arm.

'Stop a minute,' he said. 'I want to pay my respects.'

He put his face close to one of the small square panes

of glass and peered in. The window was decked out with bonnets and straw hats, veils and ribbons. To casual passers-by it all looked so pretty and dainty – they didn't know what a sweating stew of scholars was daily imprisoned in that back room.

'You can't go in that door,' gasped Pawl. 'Go round the back.'

'Why not?' said Billy airily. 'I might be a customer.'

He opened the shop door and the bell tinkled in the back. He stepped inside as Miss Griffiths came hurrying forward. Her smile of welcome froze when she saw Billy.

'What do you want back here, William Bellis?' she snapped. 'I thought I'd got rid of you for good.'

Billy felt in his right-hand pocket.

'I got something to give you, miss,' he said.

'Well, be quick about it.'

She held out her hand – and Billy placed the frog in the middle of it. He turned and shot out of the shop. Her piercing screams followed the two boys to the top of the High Street, where they parted from each other, grinning, with a satisfied handshake.

Billy and Rats turned down the steep slope of Milford Street. The Bellis family lived half-way down. Little Jen from next door was sitting on the step. She leant to one side as Billy stepped past. Jen tugged his jacket and he ruffled her black hair.

The little room was warm; the coal fire in the grate was never allowed to go out from one day to the next. Billy's mother looked up from the potatoes she was peeling at the table in the centre of the room.

'Well – how was it?'

'I've left, Mam. I've left Granny Griffiths for ever and ever, amen.'

His mam thought this was possibly irreverent, but after one look at his happy face, she began to smile too.

'Well, I said you were nearly a man, didn't I? Now you've got to make your way in the world like your father and Meic.'

Billy's eyes shone triumphantly.

'I start tomorrow at six, don't I?'

His mother's pale face lit up.

'You've got a job already?'

She worked hard, washing, cleaning and cooking. Money was always a headache, but she prided herself on never owing a penny at the end of each week. 'If the rent's paid and we have enough to eat, we'll survive.' At least they never went cold, for coal cost them nothing, since Tad and Meic worked for the Mold Colliery Company nearby. Her eyes became suddenly anxious.

'What sort of a job? Not down the pit?' A livelihood, but one to be hated and feared.

'No, not the pit. Mr Langford's taking me on at Pentre.'

'Farm work?'

'Whatever he gives me. He's always been fair. I start at tuppence a week and a half stone of potatoes.'

'That's good, Billy! Well done, son.' His mam leant over to push the kettle back over the flames. 'We'll have a cup of tea and you can tell me what he said to you.'

'Where's Sophie?'

'Out the back feeding Porcyn.'

'I'll just go and talk to her for a minute.'

Billy went through the scullery and out into the yard at the back. His eleven-year-old sister was leaning over a low wall watching Porcyn, their monster sow, in her sty. Sophie's face brightened when she saw her brother.

'I've brought her something,' he said.

He felt in his left pocket and brought out a handful of acorns he'd picked up by the river. He scattered them in front of the sow's snout. Her nostrils quivered as she scented the treat, then she gobbled them up greedily. The children laughed.

'How was school?' Billy asked.

Sophie attended the church school below the vicarage. She made a face.

'Don't want to talk about it,' she said.

So Billy told her about his job, and watched her face brighten at his good news, delighted for him.

He kept the second piece of information until later that evening, when the whole family was together. Tad and Meic had each had a wash in the tin bath in the scullery. Their dusty black pit clothes were out on the back line airing; their thick caps were stowed under the dresser. Everyone was sitting round. Mam placed the pot of steaming potatoes in the middle of the table. Billy could wait no longer. He looked at Meic, and remarked, 'I saw an empty house today.'

'Empty?' asked Meic.

'Yes, a good stone house, bigger than this,' said Billy.

Everyone stared at him. Might this be the place for Meic and Beti to live after their marriage?

'What's the rent?'

Billy shrugged, 'You'd have to ask Old Langford, it's on his land.'

'Whereabouts?'

'Up from the river bank; it's a good house with land all round; it's in the Ellyllon field.'

There was a shocked silence – then a chorus of protests.

'That haunted house, you mean?'

'They couldn't live *there*.'

'That's been deserted ever since I can remember, and before that too.'

'Are you mad, boy?'

'Haven't you heard all the stories?'

Billy stared at them, open-mouthed.

'What stories?'

'They *see* things there,' whispered Sophie.

'That Mrs Jenkins the dressmaker, for a start,' said Mam. 'She was coming home along the Chester road late one night and saw something in that field, standing on the hillock – like a man, she said it was, but glittering and shining gold. That was years ago, and everyone knows it addled her brain. She's been crazy in the head ever since.'

Tad joined in. 'There's that story my mother used to tell about a woman who'd been to fetch her husband from the Swan and he'd had a bellyful of ale –'

Mam pursed her lips, but he went on, 'Suddenly they saw this shining man, this gleaming golden man, standing on the tump. It scared the woman stiff – and scared her husband sober.'

'You wouldn't catch me going up there after dark,' said Sophie wide-eyed.

'And what would you be doing up there after dark anyway, miss?' demanded Mam.

She pushed the bowl towards Tad. 'For goodness sake start eating these potatoes before they're clay cold – and let's hear no more about ghosts and the Ellyllon field.'

Billy sank his fork into a potato. He decided not to cause more discussion by telling them that he would be starting work tomorrow close to that very spot.

3

Billy woke next morning as soon as his mother leant over and shook him. It was still dark, but he could hear the mutter of low voices downstairs – his father and brother were preparing to go on the early shift at the pit.

The kitchen was warm. Tad was sitting in his chair by the fire, pulling his boots on. Meic was packing a bag of bread and pickle into his knapsack.

They settled their pit caps on their heads and stood ready to go.

'All fit?' Tad asked, but his eyes were on Billy. 'Hope it'll be a good day, boy,' he said.

He and Meic ruffled Billy's hair, then they braced themselves to step out into the cold. The oil lamp guttered as they slammed the door behind them. There was a rhythmical tramping of boots outside, as men from the cottages further up the road made their way down past the door to the pithead.

When the two black figures had gone, the tiny room seemed suddenly lighter. Mam placed a dish of oats and hot milk in front of Billy. He ate it obediently, but he wasn't really hungry – his stomach was uneasy. He looked out of the window. The sky was lightening. He'd have to go soon, have to leave this safe warm room, and go out alone – no Mam's skirt to cling to, as on his first day at Miss Griffiths's. This was the beginning of being an adult.

He pushed back his chair and pulled on his jacket and cap. He went into the scullery and bent down to pat Rats goodbye; the terrier snuffled at him, then poked his nose sleepily under his paws again. Mam had already packed Billy's knapsack. She wrapped a long muffler round his neck and tucked it in.

'Don't fuss, Mam,' he mumbled.

She gave him a tight hug, and then opened the front door for him. Billy was taken aback when he saw her blinking back tears.

'Don't worry, Mam,' he said. 'I'll be all right. I'll only be over at Pentre. And I've worked for old Langford before.'

'Yes, but not like this,' she said.

She watched him make his way up the road past the graveyard to where Milford Street met the High Street, by St Mary's Church. When he had disappeared from sight, she sighed and went back inside to wake Sophie.

Billy tramped down the High Street in the grey morning air. The sunshine of the previous day had been followed by a cold night. The ruts of mud were hard under his thin boots. He stumbled once or twice and winced.

None of the shops was open yet, though there were lights in some of the upper windows. When he reached the horse trough at the Cross, Billy turned down the Chester road.

He began to whistle, forcing himself to remember one hymn tune after another in order to concentrate his mind. It was a way of ignoring the pain in his middle, which wasn't caused by hunger (he knew those pangs well enough), but by a more uneasy feeling somewhere inside him, like a butterchurn turning away.

Billy was beginning his seventh hymn as he walked between the fields up the hill to Pentre. On his left he passed the opening in the roadside where the men had been digging gravel the previous day, then the sudden rise of the Ellyllon hillock. He could just make out Hen Ŷ, half concealed by undergrowth, down near the river. He still thought it would be a nice place for Meic and Beti to set up home. He walked on as far as the Swan. On his right was the Pentre smithy. Stooping against the glow inside was the silhouette of blacksmith Edwards. He was stoking up the furnace so vigorously that sparks were shooting out of the chimney above the slate roof.

At last Billy reached Pentre farmhouse. Mr Langford was in the farmyard, talking in English to a man on a horse. He turned and saw Billy.

'*Bore da*, Billy,' he said, breaking into Welsh. 'I'm glad you're punctual.' He wasted no words. 'Now as it's Thursday, I've told Selwyn that I want you to help the men in the road gang until the end of the week. Then on Monday I'll start you off working with the stock.'

The stock – that meant the animals. Billy nodded

eagerly. That was what he really wanted – to work with the cowman or the shepherd, or even in the stables. He loved the great plough horses with their patient expressions. But for the moment he would have to be patient himself and work with the paupers digging gravel; it wasn't what he would have chosen for his first day at work.

The foreman, Selwyn, now came out of the stables. Billy knew the small thin man already. He was a one-time gamekeeper with a heavy limp, caused by a crack on the knee from a rifle butt, given him one dark night by an escaping poacher.

'*Bore da*,' said Selwyn. He seemed pleased to see Billy again.

He showed him where shovels and other tools were to be found, then led him off back down the road towards Mold. Billy shouldered the heavy shovel, then had to struggle to keep up, for Selwyn had a quick jerky step, in spite of his limp.

'The rest of them should be there already,' he began to explain. 'Mr Langford is one of the overseers of the parish, so he employs some of the more able-bodied paupers whenever he needs extra hands. It'll be good to have an energetic youngster like you; you can set the pace. This road job is an emergency really – the commissioners of roads say that the stretch between here and Chester is in a scandalous state, so Mr Langford's having it resurfaced. That's what the gravel's for.'

The rest of the labourers were already there, a ragged group, sheltering under the hedge. They stood up as Selwyn approached and pulled off their caps.

'Two of you fetch the barrows and tools,' he ordered, 'and when Yanto comes with the cart, load it up straight away.' He pointed at the semicircle they had cut out of the side of the slope. 'There's plenty of gravel here, so just go on digging it out.'

When the tools arrived, the men started work. One or two of them seemed to Billy almost too emaciated to use a shovel, but they all set to with whatever strength they had, to show they were worthy of hire.

A light drizzle began to fall. Selwyn hobbled over to the hedge and brought back a few old sacks. The men draped them over their heads and shoulders and continued working even more slowly. They were gaunt figures, hollow-eyed, grimy. One or two of them had boils on their face; one they called 'sergeant' had a scar across his chin and only one eye.

Billy hoped *he*'d never be a pauper with only parish relief between him and starvation. Selwyn left them to their work and sped jerkily back up the hill to the farm.

'Here, boy,' the sergeant threw him a sack. Billy put it over his head. It was slit down one side, thick and heavy, and smelt of flour. He went on shovelling. The hours passed. Yanto arrived with the cart and they threw shovelfuls of gravel into it. The muscles of Billy's arms felt as though they were burning.

The misty rain was driving sideways. They turned their backs to it. Now they were facing across the meadows to the village and St Mary's up on the opposite hilltop. Below it was the church school.

Billy thought of Sophie. He pictured her sitting among the other girls on one of the tight packed benches, repeating the lessons over and over again in English. He knew she tried to understand – she tried so hard, she even practised at home sometimes – but she found it difficult to pronounce correctly. Besides, who could she speak English to, except the schoolmaster himself? Or the vicar? No one in Milford Street spoke English, except perhaps the occasional travelling farm labourer from England. And even then, most of the men at the lodging house looking for work at harvest-time were from Ireland and had their own language; whenever they tried to speak English it never sounded like the English taught in Mold.

From along the valley came the sound of a distant hooter from the cotton mill.

'Noon,' said the sergeant with satisfaction. He beckoned to Billy to come with him, then he limped over to the fire and fed it some wood and coal from his pockets. The rest of the gang threw down their shovels and eased themselves to sit round the fire, shuffling as close as they dared to the blessed warmth. From between the blackened stones which supported the fire, they prised out the potatoes they had pushed in earlier. The hooded figures bent over their meal, feverishly tearing open the potatoes as fast as they could, gasping and blowing as they devoured the baking hot mouthfuls.

The sergeant edged out another potato and pushed it wordlessly in Billy's direction. Only his scarred eye socket was to be seen in the shadow of his head covering, but Billy sensed that this was a kindly gesture.

'Thanks,' he said. Now it was his turn. He went over

to the hedge where he had placed his knapsack. He carried his bundle over to the bonfire and sat down again. He unfolded the cloth to reveal bread, cheese and pickle. The men's eyes brightened eagerly. Billy managed to pull the bread into eight hunks. The sergeant brought out a fearsome-looking clasp knife and obliged by cutting the cheese into lumps. Billy shared it out; it seemed to go down well with the baked potatoes. He sat contentedly huddled under his damp sack. His cheeks, hands, knees and feet glowed from the heat of the flames, although his back was cold and wet. He had never felt so tired in his life. He never wanted to stand up again – and there were still six more hours to go.

4
=

Billy's first working day finished at six-thirty. Thin rain was still falling as the road gang stumbled wearily back to the barn with barrows and shovels. The paupers shuffled off to their hovels elsewhere in Mold. *At least I've got a decent home to go to*, thought Billy, pitying them and their miserable lives.

He was on the point of following them, when old Nansi the cow-woman came out of the byre. She pulled her bonnet closer round her face against the rain and lifted her skirts to wade through the farmyard mire. Then she saw Billy whom she knew, and stopped.

'Oh, *you're* the new lad, are you? How's your first day

been? Did he put you to help with the ploughing, or were you bird-scaring?'

'I'm with the road gang,' said Billy. Then he added quickly, in case she thought he was capable of nothing better, 'But only till this job's finished.'

Nansi gave him a sideways look. 'Oh, you've been working out there at the side of the Ellyllon field, eh? Well, watch out for *ellyllon* – they come in strange forms – that's all I'll say.'

She tapped the side of her weather-beaten nose with a grimy finger. *Ellyllon* were fairy folk, and didn't worry Billy one bit. He was much more scared of something like Diafol, Mr Langford's enormous bull with the evil pink-rimmed eyes. But he remembered his family's consternation about the Hen Tŷ, and the stories they'd told. He smiled reassurance at Nansi.

'We're just digging,' he said. 'We shan't be seeing any elves – or any ghosts, for that matter.'

'Don't you be so sure, boy,' said the old woman sharply. She looked round the dusky yard and pulled him into the lamplit byre.

'Let me tell you something I've told surgeon Dr Hughes many a time – he'll be my witness I'm not lying – something that'll make your hair stand on end.'

Billy waited. She folded her arms and leant eagerly towards him in the doorway, wispy grey hair falling over her bright eyes.

'When I was fifty – and I'm nearly seventy now – King George was on the throne, poor mad George, that is, and I'd already been more than forty years a dairy-maid on this very farm, so I wasn't just a flighty girl …'

78

She lowered her voice. 'I was bringing the cattle home one moonlit night – I can still remember how their breath was making clouds of silver round their heads – and we were just coming up the slope to Pentre, taking our time, past Bryn Ellyllon, when suddenly –'

Her eyes were wide, far away.

'Yes?' breathed Billy.

'When suddenly,' she went on slowly, 'the trees on the other side of the road lit up; I thought it was the light of glow-worms in the grass – but then, then, I saw –'

Billy too was wide-eyed now. 'Saw?'

'I saw a golden figure, a golden shape, a spectre, cross the Chester road and *disappear* into the bryn …'

'Oh!' Billy paled. So his family hadn't made up those stories. Here was someone who had actually seen the spectre. Then his hand flew to his mouth. 'Oh!' he said again; he had suddenly realized, that in a moment or two he had to go home in the dusk, down that very same road.

He tightened his jacket firmly round him and pulled up his collar.

'*Nos da*,' he muttered at Nansi and stepped out into the darkening farmyard.

He reached the yard gate, climbed it and gripped it while he stood listening – the shuffle and clink of cattle in the byre, the bark of a dog across the valley, faint voices in the village – and the sudden heavy drumming of his own heart.

There wasn't a soul on the road. The only lights were in the byre behind him, and up the High Street a quarter mile distant. Between the two – and the distance he had to cover – unknown blackness.

Billy took a deep breath and plunged into it. Splashing and skidding down the muddy track, he ran as he'd never run before. Formless, shapeless terrors, reared up all round him with thousands of eyes and plucking fingers. He tore down the hill, past tree shapes with their outstretched arms, past the haunted *bryn* on his right. Pale shapes moved towards him in the fields – he gasped with terror – then realized they were sheep.

His chest was heaving as he thudded up to the cross-roads in the centre of the village. He forced himself to slow down, panting, dripping with a sweat of pure fear. He leant against a wall until his heart beat more evenly, then made his way slowly, chest still heaving, up the High Street. He had never been so pleased to pass the lit-up doorways of the pubs, breathing out their familiar gusts of smoke, ale and loud conversation.

'Billy!' It was Pawl shouting across the road. He was on his way to the Leeswood Arms with a jug. Billy tried to wave back nonchalantly.

'How was it?'

Billy shrugged. What could he say? His arms were tingling like red-hot lead; his back was aching from the stoop and throw of hours of shovelling; he had been so frightened that he'd never run so fast in his life; his feet were so sodden that one of his boots was now actually coming apart; and there was a wolf in a bottomless pit of hunger screaming in his stomach. What could he say?

'Not bad, not bad, thanks,' he managed with a wave, and continued on his way with a brave step.

At last he reached home. The warmth in the little living

room enveloped him like a blanket. He threw himself down exhausted.

'Let's take off those old boots,' said his mother. Oh, what comfort to be rid of them.

She brought a bowl from the scullery and filled it with hot water from the kettle. He placed his raw feet in the bowl and closed his eyes. The cottage seemed unnaturally quiet. Usually Sophie was waiting for him; they always exchanged news of the day's happenings. And he had thought that today of all days she'd be eager to question him.

'Where's Sophie?' he asked.

His mother paused. 'Upstairs.'

'What's the matter with her?'

His mother sighed. 'She won't tell me. Something's happened at school. Go up and talk to her. See if you can make her cheer up.'

Billy dried his feet, took a lamp, and padded upstairs to his parents' bedroom. Sophie was lying face down on the bed.

'What's the matter, Sophe?'

No answer. He put his hand on her shoulder. 'It's only me, Sophe – what's happened?'

She turned over and sat up. Her face was blotchy with weeping – the usually smiling Sophie, the most cheerful member of the family. Even now, the tears began to flow again, so that she could hardly speak.

'It's the new schoolmaster, Mr Forbes. He's from England, somewhere near London – I did understand that at least. He's only been at the school since last month, but the vicar thinks so highly of him, he comes

81

in and questions us on the Catechism, and then they go into the corridor and talk and laugh – in English, of course.'

'Yes, but what's that got to do with you?'

'Well, it wasn't so bad before the summer when Mr Probert was still there. He had a Welsh mother, he knew a bit of Welsh, and when he explained things to the monitors, fair play, they knew what he meant, so then they were able to tell us what to do.'

Sophie sobbed and scrubbed at her eyes.

'But now this new schoolmaster, he doesn't know a word of Welsh, and doesn't want to, by the look of it. The monitors warned us he was going to crack down on anyone that he heard talking Welsh in school, or even in the playground – and he has.'

'But the church school has always been like that,' said Billy. He gave Sophie's thin shoulders an encouraging squeeze. 'That's why Mam sent me to Miss Griffiths, because she knew I would always be too stupid to learn much English. But you're the clever one, you're the one that learns easily. She thought it would be good for you, if you go into service, being able to speak English.'

'I do know a bit of English,' wept Sophie. 'But he wants more than that. He wants *only* English, all the time.'

'Well, you'll manage that,' said Billy. 'If you don't know how to say it in English, you'll just have to keep quiet.'

'That's w-what I thought,' hiccuped Sophie. 'But this week he's started this new punishment – I don't know how he thought it up, it's horrible. If he catches anyone alking Welsh – even in the schoolyard – he makes them wear a Welsh-Not.'

'A what?' frowned Billy. He'd not heard of this at Miss Griffiths's.

'It's a bit of wood on a string,' explained Sophie, 'and t's got W and N written on it – for 'Welsh Not' – that's o remind you that you must not, *ever*, speak Welsh.'

'That's dreadful,' said Billy. 'But don't worry, Sophe – you're one of the best pupils, you won't have to wear it.'

'That's just it – I did; I did, this afternoon!'

More bitter tears rolled down Sophie's face.

'Lizzie Jenkins just couldn't understand what she was supposed to be writing on her slate – even her mother has o tell her everything three times before she understands – and I just helped her to rub it off and start again – and one of the monitors heard me – even though I was whispering as quietly as I could, and the noise of chanting all round was deafening – and she reported me to Mr Forbes or speaking Welsh. So it had to be my turn for the Welsh-Not. I had to wear it all the rest of the afternoon.'

'And even worse,' she sobbed, 'if you're the last one wearing it when the hometime bell's rung, you're the one that's punished.'

'You were punished?'

'He was going to cane me, but I was in such a state, he relented, and said my scholastic record had been good up to now – at least, I *think* that's what he was saying – so he said I could learn a verse of the Bible instead.'

Billy hugged her fiercely.

'I'll help you learn it,' he said. 'I'll help you get it by heart.'

83

'I know it already,' she said. She leant against him, quieter now, and recited in English:

'Though I speak with the tongues of men and of angels, and have not charity, I am become as sounding brass, or a tinkling cymbal.'

'Sounds right to me,' said Billy admiringly. 'Now come downstairs, there's a good girl; Mam's made a pot of tea, and I've so much to tell you.'

Sophie gripped his arm.

'But Billy, don't tell Mam,' she said. 'Whatever you do, don't tell Mam. It was so humiliating. I can't bear her to know about it.'

Billy shook his head in concern.

'You can't keep it quiet for long,' he said. 'You know she'll hear about it. The other children will tell it at home – you know the way word gets round.'

Sophie began to weep again.

'Oh, I was so ashamed,' she cried. She flung her apron up over her face and sobbed as though her heart would break.

Billy stood up and stared helplessly at his sister.

'I'll go and have my cup of tea anyway,' he muttered, then clattered back downstairs with raging anger in his heart.

5

During that evening the rain stopped. Overnight, along the North Wales coast, the temperature dropped. When Billy woke, the cold in the bedroom cut his face like a knife.

'Time to get up, son,' his mother was saying, placing a candle by the bed.

He lay in his warm cocoon a minute or two longer. It was still dark outside, but the flickering candle-light sparkled on glittering patterns of ferns and swirls on the inside of the window. It was Jack Frost's first visit of the winter; Billy felt strangely excited.

He shivered, then shot out of bed and dressed himself as quickly as his chill fingers would allow. He crept downstairs so as not to wake his sister.

'I've put in some extra bacon and bread,' said his mother as she packed his food tin. 'It's bad enough being on relief at the best of times, but in this weather …' She shook her head in sad sympathy. 'I don't know how they find the strength to lift a shovel.'

'I was the best worker of them all yesterday,' boasted Billy.

'And so you should be, boy!' she exclaimed. 'You, a healthy lad, all of ten years old, and them poor strays and starvelings.'

Billy ate his breakfast, then stood up. His mother helped to wind his muffler round him, and did his jacket up to the neck.

'Here,' she said, giving him two small parcels wrapped in rags. 'I've had these potatoes in the ashes. They'll warm your hands – you always get such bad chilblains.'

'Thanks, Mam,' said Billy.

He put one in each pocket of his jacket. Then he swung his knapsack over his shoulder, picked up the tea jack, heavy with its weight of cold tea, and whistled to Rats.

'Rats! Come on, come on, boy – walkies.'

'You can't take that dog to work,' said Billy's mother in shocked tones.

'Yes, I can, Selwyn said I could, as long as the men aren't prevented from working. He said it would keep the men cheerful, and if they were cheerful, they would work with more of a will.'

Billy stood on the doorstep, surveying Milford Street. Everything lay under a thick white layer of frost. Even the still air seemed veiled in white. As he hurried along, trying not to slip, he was glad his jacket had once been Meic's, and was still too long for him. The sleeves hung down and protected his raw wrists somewhat from the cold. The warm potatoes in his pockets radiated comfort. It was good to have Rats trotting beside him too.

They soon left the village behind and made their way along the turnpike road to Chester. The countryside around was white and still. The sheep stood in the fields like white mounds. Billy felt ashamed of his stupid fancies of the night before.

He reached the gravel cutting below Bryn Ellyllon. Most of the raggedy men were already there, standing backs to the wind, stamping their feet and clamping their mottled hands under their armpits for warmth. Billy nodded at some of them. He was beginning to connect a few names with faces.

'That yours?' asked an old man with a wrinkled rosy face like a stored apple. That was Ebenezer. He was looking at Rats with his habitual expression of slightly anxious puzzlement.

'Yes, that's Rats.' Then, as though answering an objection, Billy added, 'He never takes notice of sheep; he's a ratter. Good 'un, too.'

Close to Ebenezer, docile, stood a large young man with a pale vague face. He was known as Drownded. The others had to pull him along by the hand, or nudge him to get him working. His thoughts – if he had any – were clearly elsewhere.

'Why's he called Drownded?' Billy had whispered to the sergeant.

'Because he fell into the Alyn when he was a babby. They hauled him out by the seat of his breeches, but he's been vacant-like ever since.'

He raised his voice and prodded Drownded. 'Been vacant-like, ever since, haven't you, *bach*?'

The young man nodded obediently, and some of the others guffawed.

Then there was Pigtail, quite a young man, who had been a sailor, until a fall from the rigging onto the deck of a Liverpool vessel had invalided him out of the navy. His parents had died while he was at sea, so he had begged his way round the coast as far as Chester.

'And before I knew it, I was in Wales,' he laughed.

'They were that good to me at the farms I called at, I decided to stay. So I'm a Welshie by adoption.'

In fact, he spoke – at quite a rate of knots – a very odd sort of Welsh–Liverpool mixture, which made people smile. Then they noticed his stiff leg and the scars on his face and were sorry for him. He winked at Billy now and said, 'Decided to stay on another day then, have you, boy?'

Billy smiled in reply, hugging and slapping himself with his hands to keep out the cold.

'It's worse at sea,' said Pigtail cheerfully, 'when your hands freeze to the shrouds, and the tears in your eyes turn to drops of ice.'

A man with a bush of curly grey hair was standing with his head on one side, his eyes fixed intently on the speaker's face. Pigtail took a deep breath and bellowed at him, 'Things could be worse!'

Jac nodded uncomprehendingly. He was completely deaf, though managing to make clear what he wanted by means of his expressive black eyes and quick gestures. He hitched up the string which held his coat tight round his middle and pulled a bottle from an inside pocket. He took a drink, then offered it to Billy, who refused politely.

Rats was trotting round the group, getting to know them. He stopped in front of two men who leant forward peering at him, then made a great fuss of him. Amos and Jeremiah were identical twins, slight, wiry men. They had such feeble eyesight that they were frequently seen in Mold hurrying along arm in arm, partly for companionship, partly for safety's sake.

Yanto arrived with the tools in the back of the cart, pulled by Doli, the small bay mare. They made a start. Rats went off to sniff and explore the hedge-bottom where there was less frost under his paw pads than in the open fields. By now the sun had come up, and was floating low in the sky like a brilliant orange ball. It was still bitterly cold.

Mr Langford rode down the slope towards them. He stood and watched their slow progress for a while. The shovelfuls of gravel crashed more frequently into the cart as the men worked on with heightened zeal. Then he dismounted and came over to them. He pointed his whip at the cutting in the gravel bank.

'We've taken out enough,' he said. 'We've filled in all the pot-holes in the road between here and the parish boundary. That should last until the spring floods, at least. Now I'd like this cutting filled in, so the field can be levelled off. I'm thinking of ploughing it next autumn, so make this the last cartload.'

'What shall we use for infill, sir?' asked the sergeant.

'You can take the top of the tump and throw it down into the cutting. That will do two jobs at the same time. It will level off the tump – it's always been a hindrance to the ploughing anyway – and with this cutting filled in, we can neaten the side of the road again and put in a stout new fence. I'll come back later and see how you're getting on with the infill,' he said, swinging himself up into the saddle.

An hour later Yanto led Doli away with the last load. The men leant wearily on their shovels. They looked at one another, then at the frost covered tump. It rose up from the edge of the road to the height of a man, like some shape moulded by the hand of a giant. This October day its grassy slopes were sparkling white. It would be hard work.

'We'll never get into that,' said Pigtail. 'It'd be like cutting stone with a butter knife.'

Jac took a quick swig at his bottle.

'I can't do no more,' gasped old Ebenezer. His face peered out from his muffler in a rosy round of misery. 'My toes is dropping off.'

They all glanced at his rag-bound feet. Billy felt much the same; he'd never been so cold. Even Rags was unhappy now, sitting under the hedge, whimpering.

Jac held his stomach and contorted his face to show that he was desperate for food and incapable of using a shovel a moment longer. He rolled his eyes longingly towards the fire.

'All right, all right,' agreed the sergeant. 'At ease!'

They threw down their shovels and crowded over to the fire. At that moment they became aware of Selwyn jerkily hurrying down the road.

'Master's changed his mind. Says it's too cold – you can have a half day. Start again tomorrow.'

But the next day was equally cold, and so was the following week. Stories reached Mold of the Dee being frozen over. Old people died of pneumonia. The body of a tramp was found, white with frost, leaning upright against a tree on the Denbigh road. Mr Langford's road gang was laid off for a week. No wages.

Billy chafed at the delay. He had stopped contributing – however little – to the household. He felt ashamed

90

when he heard the slam of the door and the sound of boots going down the street early each morning, as his father and brother set off for the pit as usual. So he helped his mother about the house, carried water – when the pump wasn't frozen solid – slipped and slid to do the shopping for her in the village, heard Sophie's lessons after school, and saw to Porcyn, whose last days at the trough were fast approaching.

6

At last the temperature rose again, as suddenly as it had dropped.

'October the eleventh,' said Billy's mother, looking at the pedlar's calendar. 'Just think, Billy, it's two weeks since you started work.'

'And left Granny Griffiths, for ever and ever, glory halleluia,' said Billy.

He swung off to work whistling, with Rats trotting at his side. He greeted the road gang like old friends; he hadn't seen any of them for nearly two weeks. Drownded fell on Rats with a cry of recognition and lifted him up to hug him, crooning lovingly.

'Where's old Ebenezer?' asked Billy suddenly, looking round.

No one answered. Jac rolled his eyes and made a thumb's down gesture. Pigtail cleared his throat.

'Didn't you hear?' he said casually. 'It was his feet

took him – frozen to the knee. Gangrene it was – he only lasted three days. Soon over. He's being buried today, now they can open the ground.'

Billy swallowed. No one so well known to him had ever died before.

The cart creaked down the road.

'Whoa, Doli,' cried Yanto.

Selwyn jumped down and came hobbling over with his jerky gait. He rubbed his hands together.

'Right boys,' he said to the group round the fire. 'You're nigh on two weeks behind. We've waited days for this, now let's get going.'

He gave instructions to the sergeant, then hauled himself up next to Yanto. They drove off. The road gang took their spades and scrambled up to the top of the tump. First they attacked all the gorse bushes and tipped them over the edge of the hillock. The sergeant dragged them by the roots and threw them on the fire, where they blazed up brightly.

Then the men laid bare the turf on top of the tump. Drownded, Jac and Elwyn wobbled off with the wheelbarrows and tipped the contents into the cutting. There was soon a rhythmical chain going: the men at the top loosened the mixture of soil and pebbles and threw it down into the barrows, which the three men on the level ground lower down wheeled away and tipped. The cutting began to fill up. Few words were exchanged as the men concentrated on what they were doing. After two or three hours, a couple of hundred barrow loads had been taken away and tipped into the deep inlet.

'Phew,' said the sergeant. 'I need a breather. Stand at ease.'

They stood where they were, leaning on their spades, and took deep breaths.

Jac pulled out a bottle, looked at it, tipped it upside down, put it like a telescope to his eye, then turned it upside down again. Not a drop. He shrugged and threw the bottle into the hedge. There was a silence, broken only by the sergeant's wheezing chest.

Then Elwyn, an emaciated old man with an empty clay pipe permanently clamped between his gums, took a spade and experimentally pushed it into the side of the tump. It made a dull thudding noise, and the blade could make no entry.

'Stone,' he said laconically.

'We could break it up with the sledge-hammers,' suggested Pigtail.

The diggers dug away more of the topsoil. It trickled and fell away gradually until a score or more barrowloads had been removed. They scraped away more of the soil and pebbles and a good-sized flat boulder was revealed.

'Some stone, Elwyn,' said the sergeant sarcastically. 'The sledge-hammer wouldn't be no good. Now heave-ho, boys – we'll have to move that out of the way if the master's thinking of ploughing this field. You might as well tip it into the pit, anything to fill it up quick, so's we finish the job.'

They threw off their jackets and mufflers and set to, sweating and grunting as they strained to push and roll the enormous boulder six or eight yards to the edge of the field. At last it lay alongside the hedge-bottom.

'Phew,' gasped Pigtail, his chest heaving. 'I'm not the man I was at twenty-five.' He glanced down momentarily at his leg.

The sound of a single bell suddenly echoed across the meadows from the parish church, startling them.

'Ebenezer,' whispered the twins in unison, tugging off their caps and flattening them to their chest. The others – then Billy, copying them – did the same. Not hearing the solemnly tolling bell, Jac glanced round and looked puzzled. Billy mouthed 'Ebenezer,' at him, then made bell-ringing gestures, and a thumb's down sign. Jac's face lit up with understanding, and he gravely pulled off his cap too. They stood with bowed heads for a moment or two. The sergeant straightened himself briskly.

'Come on, now boys, let's get on. We seem to have the lid off the tump, so it should be easier going now. Billy lad, stand on the top and chip away at the loose soil at the edge.'

'Right,' said Billy, and scrambled up to the top.

Hearing his voice, Rats raced up behind him and ran round the top of the hillock, barking with excitement. Suddenly, he stopped and began to dig furiously, sending out such a spray of dirt and stones that Billy had to shield his face with his arm.

'Stop it, Rats!' he laughed. 'Go off down to the river. Stop that, you stupid mutt!'

Rats seemed to understand and raced off, slithering and sliding down the side of the hillock.

'He had something in his jaws,' said Jeremiah.

'What did you give him?' asked Amos.

'I didn't give him nothing,' said Billy.

'Bone,' said Elwyn. 'He had a bone.'

'I didn't give him a bone,' said Billy. 'Where'd he get it from?'

'Dead sheep, most likely,' suggested Pigtail.

They nodded, satisfied, and bent to their work again. The bell had stopped tolling. The rhythmical sounds of digging, filling, trundling and tipping filled their ears. The hillock had been considerably reduced in height by now. Many large stones had been thrown into the pit. Two more very large boulders were removed with much difficulty from the sides. Occasionally there was a cracking sound as their spades smashed into bits of old crocks. Instead of dirt and pebbles, they were now digging up a mixture of burnt material and fragments of red pottery.

'Someone's rubbish tip,' grunted the sergeant.

Suddenly, Drownded stopped digging and gazed down at the ground in front of him. He let out a fearful screech, dropped his spade and covered his mouth with his enormous hands.

'What is it? what's the matter?' cried Billy. 'Drownded, what is it?'

He followed the direction of Drownded's stare of horror, and started back himself as he realized what he was seeing. Half uncovered in the dirt was a human skull.

Drownded, Billy, the sergeant and Elwyn stood stock-still and stared.

'If that's what I think it is,' breathed the sergeant, 'there's more of him under there.'

Drownded moaned with fear and stepped back. The

rest of the gang had left their barrows and run closer to peer up and over the top of the flattened hillock.

'A body, a body ...' they whispered, looking at one another. Who had buried it here? Why wasn't it buried in the parish graveyard? Had it been secretly buried after some foul play? Who was it? There was something here they didn't understand – or like. One or two of them shivered. The sergeant took charge.

'Don't touch anything more,' he ordered. 'I'd best get Mr Langford.'

He set off uphill towards Pentre farm. The others stood staring at the half-uncovered, rounded brownish object. There was no doubting that it was a skull, a human skull.

7

Within ten minutes Mr Langford was trotting down towards them, the sergeant panting behind. The farmer dismounted and strode up to the top of the hillock. The men made way for him. One glance was enough.

'Yes, that's a skull,' he said. 'You'd better dig on carefully and see what remains of the body. Sergeant, you dig alone. Stand back, men. Give him room.'

The men shuffled back a step or two, watching breathlessly. No one noticed Mary Edwards, the blacksmith's wife, walking along the road from Pentre to Mold. She saw the dozen or so labourers circling the crown of the hillock. They were gazing intently inwards like mourners round a graveside. She wondered what was holding their attention.

The sergeant had just carefully uncovered the rest of the skull. It lay there, eye-sockets staring at the sky. There was a pause.

'Gently now,' said Mr Langford.

Billy stared, his heart thumping. With the tip of his spade, the sergeant pushed away more soil. There was a quantity of little round objects mixed up with the dirt.

'Marbles,' whispered Billy.

'No, son, they're beads,' said Pigtail.

Mr Langford stared into the hole.

'Gather them up and keep them all together,' he ordered.

Billy hesitated, then bent down and quickly picked up as many of the beads as he could see, trying to keep his fingers away from where the skull still lay. Jac was making unmistakable gestures to the group that these must be the remains of a *woman*. Billy placed the beads on one of the shovels, then hastily wiped his fingers on his jacket.

'There's quite a quantity,' said Mr Langford. 'Enough to fill a panmug, I should say. Are there more?'

The sergeant uncovered a little further. There were some barely recognizable shreds of coarse cloth, which he pushed to one side. Then a piece of thin metal came into view. They all peered forward.

'It's a bit of tin,' said Jeremiah.

'A bit of an old tin chest,' suggested Amos.

They drew in their breath. What might it contain?

Treasure? Coins? Her last will and testament? They watched open-mouthed. Even Drownded, keeping well behind Pigtail, couldn't take his eyes off the sight. Mr Langford gingerly pulled up one side of the piece of tin and the sergeant scraped out more dirt.

''T'aint a chest, Amos Prothero,' said Elwyn in disappointed tones. ''Tis only a piece of metal, folded under like.'

Working delicately with the tip of his spade, the sergeant next uncovered several small knobbly pieces … of something. They drew in their breath. More beads? Jewels? He wiped them on his breeches.

'Bones,' said Elwyn.

'Bits of her backbone!' breathed Pigtail.

'Vertebrae,' said Mr Langford. 'Human.'

'Is there any more of her?' asked Elwyn, putting his pipe in his pocket in order to concentrate more closely.

'Let's have a look under here,' said Mr Langford. He took hold of the piece of tin, glanced at it dismissively, wiggled it free of the soil, and threw it across into the hedge. The men leant forward again over the grave. A few more vertebrae were found, a few more beads. They were all laid carefully to one side.

The sergeant dug on for quarter of an hour or more, but nothing further was found apart from more burnt remains – some of it now identified as bone – mixed up with broken bits of red earthenware. This rubbish was all wheeled away and dumped in the pit. Mr Langford straightened himself up and glanced at the skull and backbones.

'Put them in one of the wheelbarrows and cover them

up for now,' he ordered. 'She's been under there since long before our time. She should be laid to rest. This is vicar's work. I'll go and give him a full account of this … incident … myself. Meanwhile,' he glanced round at the wide-eyed men, 'you're to keep this strictly to yourselves. No need for this to get about and cause upset. Do you hear me?'

Catching Jac's eye, he repeated slowly to him, 'Do – not – tell – anyone,' and waggled his finger at him. Jac nodded solemnly to show he understood. Mr Langford looked round from one to the next, and said, 'Not a word, neither in the Swan, nor the Bull, nor the Leeswood Arms, nor the Black Lion, the Dolphin, the Miners' Arms, the Crown –'

'No, sir; not in the Feathers neither, nor the King's Head, nor the Star,' they prompted him. '*No, sir!*'

He glared at them.

'No, nor anywhere – do you hear?'

The men nodded earnestly. The noon siren sounded from the cotton mill along the Alyn. For once they had forgotten the time. Mr Langford came over to the fire with the shovelful of dull-looking brown beads. He scraped the dirt off one or two of them. They looked no brighter.

'Not precious stones then,' he said in a disappointed tone.

He placed a few of them on a flat stone and hit them gently with one of the sledge-hammers. They seemed soft and cracked apart easily into fragments of clear brownish-orange glass. He put a few more onto the shovel and pushed it into the fire. There was a sudden glow in the flames. When he withdrew the shovel, Billy could see a pool of orange liquid on it, just like his mother's treacle toffee before it set. A fragrant smell rose from the liquid.

'Resin,' said Mr Langford in resigned tones. He pocketed a few of the beads for curiosity's sake, leaving the rest lying by the fire. He called the sergeant over.

'I must get to see the vicar about this, then I'll go back to the house. There's a deal to do: the heifers are to be judged tomorrow. And that reminds me,' he turned to Billy, 'as soon as this road job is finished, I want you to start work helping with the stock.'

Billy's face lit up.

'Yessir!' he exclaimed. This was what he had been waiting for all this time. Mr Langford smiled at his enthusiasm. He turned back to the others.

'Right, men,' he said, 'carry on filling the pit this afternoon. Sergeant, you might as well bring that bit of tin back to the house later; it may shed some light on the poor woman's death. If not, it can go to the rag-and-bone man. Now remember, men, this is to go no further.'

Within a quarter of an hour, Mary Edwards returned from doing her errands in Mold. When she saw that Mr Langford was no longer with the road gang, she went across to Jeremiah and Amos, her cousins, as they ate their bread and cheese by the fire, and asked them how they were. Why were they altering the look of the place by flattening Bryn Ellyllon, which had stood between Pentre and Mold since her great-grandfather's time at least? And why had they all been gathered round on the top of it – had it been a prayer meeting? Being a forceful and persistent person, Mary Edwards soon elicited a response – at first reluctant, then in considerable and grisly detail; she was even allowed – on pain of death if she told anyone – a peek under the cover of the wheelbarrow.

Within half an hour, she had hurried back with news of the finding of the bones and the beads to her husband's smithy, where it greatly interested his customers waiting for their horses to be shod. From the smithy the item of news was carried red-hot to David Lewis, the toll-gatekeeper – who always shared any gossip with passers-by – and thence to John Jones, the Pentre nailer, to Sarah Bellis (a distant cousin of Billy's tad) who kept the Bull, to Evan Hughes, the Pentre butcher, and his son, Edward, and to John Challinor and his wife who kept the Swan. When John Langford returned from seeing the vicar, his wife Rebecca greeted him with: 'What's all this about finding a body?'

8

Meanwhile, the men were taking an extended meal break. They were animated for once, talking about the body – or lack of it – and speculating on how the woman could have met her death. Billy looked round for Rats and held out a piece of meat pie for him. But the little dog remained sitting still under the hedge, yelping piteously.

'What's the matter, old lad?' called Billy. 'Come on – come and have a bit of Mam's mutton pie.'

But Rats continued whimpering and wouldn't budge.

'I'd better go and see what it is,' said Billy to the others. He took his food tin and tea jack over to the hedge and sat down next to Rats. The terrier was biting feverishly at one of his front paws. Billy examined it and found a small piece of metal which had sunk deeply into one of Rat's pads. Billy pulled the metal out gently between his teeth and pushed it in his pocket. Then he poured a few drops of cold tea onto the pad to wash it. Rats wagged his tail gratefully and changed his mind about the mutton pie.

Billy wedged himself comfortably against a gnarled hawthorn trunk. He sat back, munching contentedly, with one arm round the little dog's warm body. His other arm was uncomfortable; something was poking into it. He saw that it was the folded piece of tin which Mr Langford had thrown into the hedge.

Billy looked at it curiously. It was a strip about a foot wide, and probably about four feet long if it was opened out – but the two ends had been doubled back under. The metal was very soft and thin, and it bent easily. In some places it was split and squashed; some cracked bits were hanging loose. It was a scrap of this which Rats had trodden on. Billy gingerly took a handful of grass and wiped some of the dirt off the surface of the metal.

'There's bumpy patterns on it,' he remarked to Rats, and rubbed a little harder. 'Squares and circles, and patterns like hobnails, and cords, and cough lozenges. And look, someone's punched holes all the way along the two long edges.'

Rats came round to sniff at it. Billy poured out a few

more drops of his cold tea to wet the surface of the metal and rubbed it again with his cuff. The raised surface began to gleam slightly, a soft yellowish gleam.

'That ain't tin,' thought Billy, 'more like ... copper, perhaps?' Like the great pans and pudding moulds he'd seen hanging up in the kitchen of the Pentre farm. He considered the yellowish polished area again.

'No,' he said to Rats. 'It's more like the candlesticks on our mantelpiece. It must be bronze.'

Pigtail's voice suddenly broke in.

'Hey, Billy lad,' he called. 'You'll perish over there. Come and have a warm.'

Billy reluctantly left what he was doing and returned to the group round the fire.

'That bit of tin Mr Langford threw away –' he began.

'Oh, lawks,' said the sergeant, smacking his forehead. 'I meant to take it back to the house. Where is it?'

'Over there,' said Billy, pointing – but it had gone. Rats was racing away across the field, dragging the bumping, tearing bit of metal after him.

'That danged dog's got it. Get him back here!' ordered the sergeant.

He and Billy leapt to their feet.

'Rats – here boy!'

The terrier dropped his booty and barked joyfully as Billy ran towards him; this could be a good game. Rats pounced on the strip of metal again and worried it, then dragged it away before Billy could arrive.

'Rats! Drop it!' shouted Billy. 'Do you hear me? Drop it!'

He was growing angry and embarrassed. He caught

up with the little terrier eventually, at the far side of Cae Ellyllon, near Pentre mill. He grabbed at Rats, who shot away, leaving the metal lying on the ground. Billy picked it up and hoisted it under his arm.

'Yoo-hoo! You, boy,' came a voice.

Martha Lewis, the miller's wife, and niece of the toll-gatekeeper, was waving eagerly at him across her washing line. 'Come here a minute.'

'I've got to go back …' faltered Billy.

But she came running across, pegs in her hand, skirts billowing.

'Oh, I shan't keep you a minute,' she said. 'Just tell me, quick now – is it right you men have dug up a body? In a shallow grave, wasn't it? How was she done in?'

Billy stared. How in heaven's name had she found out already? Then he suddenly remembered Mr Langford's strictures and was struck dumb. He mustn't say a word. But how could he refuse to answer? Especially someone as forceful as red-faced, roly-poly Mrs Lewis.

'Er … M-Mr … L-Langford knows all a-b-bout it,' he managed to stutter.

Then he turned and ran, hurdling the thistles and tussocks till he arrived panting, back at the fire. He handed the piece of metal over to the sergeant. The men stopped talking and looked at it. The patch that Billy had polished glowed yellowish in the pale gleams of the afternoon sun.

'That's never tin,' breathed Elwyn.

'No, by thunder,' whispered Pigtail. 'That's gold, boys, that's gold.'

9

'Gold!'

They stood and stared, until Elwyn suggested eventually, 'Open it out. Let's see the length of it.'

The sergeant bent back the two sides, so that they could see the full length of the piece of metal. The embossed patterns running from end to end stood out on the surface. It curved slightly, and one side seemed longer than the other.

'What's that you got there then?' came a voice behind them.

Heads turned with a guilty start.

'Oh, 'tis only you, Yanto,' said Jeremiah angrily. 'What do you want to come creeping up like that for?'

'I wasn't creeping up, Jeremiah Pugh. I'm going to town for the mistress, so I thought I'd just stop by and have a peek at this body you found.'

'It ain't a body – it's a skull and some bits of bone,' said the sergeant. 'Master's gone to tell vicar about it.'

'And so what's that then?' persisted Yanto, pointing at the piece of metal.

'Oh … oh … er … just … er …' The sergeant's imaginative powers failed completely.

'Just a bit of old metal we found,' said Pigtail airily.

Yanto put his head on one side.

'Funny shape,' he said. 'Like a sort of horse cloth. It'd fit over Doli's shoulders, that would.'

They considered, looking across at the little bay mare

cropping the grass, then back at the metal shape.

'Mmm,' admitted the sergeant. 'It would, I suppose.'

Some of the men murmured in agreement; perhaps it had been some sort of horse tack. Amos peered at it short-sightedly.

'Perhaps she was killed falling off her horse,' he suggested.

No one had time to comment, for at that moment there was the sound of heavy footsteps running towards them over the grass, accompanied by the sound of wheezing. They were joined by the miller's wife – a shawl hastily flung over her washing apron – and her neighbour, Mrs Challinor, from the Swan.

'We just wanted to see the body,' said Mrs Lewis breathlessly.

'Well, you can't, Martha Lewis,' snapped the sergeant.

'And they found this too,' said Yanto, pointing at the metal object. 'With the body, was it, boys?'

The road gang stood by helplessly.

'And Mrs Langford's Nansi said there was beads too!' said Mrs Challinor.

The men involuntarily glanced at the grass near the fire. Martha Lewis swooped down with a triumphant cry.

'Here, look, Cathy, here's some – here, you get one too.'

The two women fell to their knees, feeling feverishly in the grass for beads.

'I wouldn't mind one for my missus,' said Elwyn suddenly. He thrust his pipe in his pocket and crouched down, feeling round in the grass.

'An' so would I, come to that,' said Yanto, who had an

ailing wife. 'Give her something to talk about.'

He too bent over and peered at the ground.

Billy's heart was burning. He would dearly love to take one of the dirty beads home to show the family. But Mr Langford was his employer, the tenant of the field. Would it be stealing? How about one? Only one bead; not out of greed, just curiosity. He put his hand on the grass and felt about. Suddenly his palm felt a solid object, one of the beads. He stood up, pocketing it swiftly.

The members of the road gang were left staring at the piece of metal lying on the sergeant's outstretched hands.

'I wouldn't mind a bit of *this* to remember the day by,' said Pigtail. He looked at it greedily. 'Especially if it's gold –'

'We could take off a little cracked bit,' suggested Jeremiah timidly.

'Just a corner,' nodded Amos, fingering one of the edges. 'Look – there's a bit missing there already.'

'No!' said Drownded suddenly. He clasped his hands against his chest. 'No! Thou shalt not steal.'

They stared at him, horrified and ashamed. He spoke so seldom, that when he did, it was all the more forceful.

'Quite right, Drownded, quite right – you've learnt your lessons well at Chapel,' said the sergeant heartily, though his eyes still lingered longingly on the yellowish patch of metal. 'Though if it *is* gold, it's worth enough to keep us in beer and baccy for the rest of our days. Just think of the sovereigns you could get out of this!'

'Hey, mister, what've you got?'

Children, just released from school, came swarming

into the field, attracted by the sight of people hunting for something in the grass – if it wasn't mushrooms, what was it? The sound of their shouts and calls was followed by the creaking of a cart coming down the Pentre slope.

'Sarah Williams,' said Elwyn admiringly. 'She's like clockwork that woman – Tuesdays and Fridays – fifteen mile to Chester, fifteen mile back – never a minute out.'

Billy knew Sarah Williams. Her carrier's yard and stable were at the back of the High Street. She was a large florid woman with a filthy temper. She was afraid of no one, and had been known to drive other carts into the ditch if they didn't give way. Her customers, however, always felt completely safe in her care, knowing she would protect them whatever happened.

Now she called 'Whoa!', halted the cart, and made an unprecedented stop, allowing three people to dismount. Then with a brisk 'Gee up,' and flick of the whip, she urged the horse forwards again. Two men and a woman, returned from shopping in Chester, came hurrying across, questions pouring from their mouths before they were even within earshot.

'We heard all about it from old David Lewis at the toll gate. Can we see the body? How was she killed? Were there any other bodies there? How long has she been buried? Was it that red-haired woman that disappeared from Gwernymynydd last April?'

Meanwhile, the children were dancing round the group, playing with sticks in the fire, searching for something – whatever there was – in the grass, running up and down the sides of the flattened tump, and leaping in and out of the nearly full pit.

The sergeant decided that discipline was needed. He placed the metal on the outstretched arms of Jac, Drownded and Billy, and turned to glare at the children.

'*Away*, you little beggars, *away*!' he shouted. 'Or I'll get the constable! *You*, Huw Beynon – I know you – I'll tell your father, he'll leather you! And you, Davies boy – yes, you – I know where you live. *Be off*!'

As the children scattered, he turned to the other onlookers. 'And ladies and gentlemen, may I respectfully remind you that this is Mr Langford's field, and any requests for intelligence about this field or its contents should be addressed to him at Pentre farm.'

The spectators backed away, but only as far as the edge of the field. They were soon joined by others from the directions of both Pentre and Mold. Then Selwyn came hobbling down the road and across to the gang. He took command. He set Pigtail, Elwyn and Billy to stand guard over the still-covered wheelbarrow of bones.

'And I'll take that bit of old tin back to the master,' he said. 'I clean forgot it before.'

'Oh-ah, I'll come with you,' said the sergeant eagerly. He didn't want to let it from his sight.

'Come with me? You gone soft, sergeant?' said Selwyn. 'I expect I can manage to carry it without help – even with my leg.'

He glared at the sergeant and hobbled away with the squashed piece of metal under one arm.

Later that afternoon, the vicar and Mr Langford rode

over to the men. The farmer spoke in a low voice.

'The sooner we get this business settled, the quicker we can set this field to rights. It's just a nine-days' wonder – you know what people are like. It's time these bones were decently buried. How about that soft patch of ground by the drainage ditch? Sergeant, would you take the vicar over there?'

The old soldier fixed the vicar with his sound eye, and nodded.

'Follow us with the barrow, boy,' he instructed Billy.

The sergeant set off across the grass, with his spade over his shoulder. He was followed by the vicar on his horse, then by Billy trundling the barrow after them as fast as he could. As he steered a wavering course around tussocks and muddy grass, he had to jerk the tarpaulin occasionally to keep the contents of the barrow covered. The skull and bones slid about in the bottom of the barrow. Billy began to feel responsible for the person this once had been. He tried to push the barrow more gently, out of respect.

He caught up with the other two. They had stopped, and the sergeant was digging with as much speed as possible, throwing the soil into a mound at the side of the hole.

When it was about four feet deep, the vicar nodded.

'That'll do, sergeant,' he said. He pointed at the barrow. 'Lay them in.'

Billy lifted the tarpaulin. The old soldier cleaned his palms on his breeches and gingerly took hold of the skull. He knelt and reached down with one arm, placing the skull in the bottom of the hole. Then he carefully took the other bones and laid them round it.

The vicar dismounted and handed the reins to Billy, then his tall hat. He pulled a pair of spectacles and a black bound book from his pocket. The sergeant scrambled to his feet breathlessly, pulled off his tattered hat and leant on his spade. Billy remembered old Ebenezer; he pulled off his cap too, and bowed his head. The sergeant looked sideways at the vicar.

'We don't know as she … er … he was a Christian,' he said.

The vicar gazed back at him over his spectacles.

'He or she was certainly one of God's children,' he said mildly, 'and I shall bury him or her appropriately.'

He opened the book and began to read, in English. The prayers went on for quite a long time. Billy tried hard to catch the meaning.

'*We brought nothing into this world, and it is certain we can carry nothing out,*' intoned the vicar. Billy nodded to himself. This poor old skeleton had been dressed in his or her best, with gold and jewels and things, but they'd all been left behind when it had died. And now people were squabbling over them.

All the same, Billy was glad he'd picked up one of those dirty old beads. It wasn't as though he was going to keep it, or sell it. It was for Sophie. To make her happy. She'd never had any jewellery before in her life. He knew she'd treasure it – even if it had been buried for … how long?

'*A thousand years in thy sight are but as yesterday,*' read the vicar, and Billy understood that too.

Eventually the black book was quietly closed.

'Amen,' said the vicar. 'Amen, amen,' echoed the other two.

The horse moved its hooves restlessly, while Billy shovelled the mound of earth back into the hole. Then the vicar mounted and trotted back in the direction of St Mary's, leaving the sergeant and Billy to tread solemnly over the surface of the freshly dug patch.

10

'Treasure trove!'

Information about the find spread so quickly, it was as though the inhabitants of Mold were breathing the news from the very air. Everyone suddenly felt the need to view the field – even though they were as familiar with it as their own back yard. Hats, mufflers, shawls and clogs were hastily put on, and a constant stream of visitors hurried along the Chester road. There they stood and stared at Bryn Ellyllon – or the flattened hillock which was all that was left of it.

The trampled muddy field, the filled-in cutting, were viewed with awe and speculation from a distance of ten yards, which was as near as Mr Langford's men would allow spectators. In the following days, many a keen gardener in the neighbourhood began to dig over his patch with renewed vigour and hope – reasoning with himself that in October he always turned over the soil anyway – and if he *should* hit upon something interesting buried in the ground, then all the better …

On Sunday, 13 October, the Welsh chapels and St Mary's Church were full. Billy and Sophie sat with their mother in the church. The stone floor flags were cold, and the great metal stove, crackling away, did not raise the temperature for those sitting frozen in the pews. Billy's fingers played with the bead in his pocket; he still hadn't found the right moment to give it to Sophie. *Surely* he hadn't stolen it? After all, Mr Langford hadn't set much store by the beads. Billy looked up at his favourite stone angel at the top of a pillar. He wondered whether angels could see into pockets … There was excited anticipation in the air. Several ladies were wearing new bonnets in honour of the occasion. Surely the vicar couldn't ignore the discovery of mounds of skeletons, chests full of jewels, a hoard of gold … He would have to preach on the Find – wouldn't he?

He did, but briefly. He stood leaning over the pulpit, white-whiskered, rosy-cheeked. He beamed at them, then began to speak. The Welsh speakers among his congregation concentrated hard, so as to understand his English sermon.

He said he wanted to allay people's fears – nothing untoward had happened. It appeared that the tump they called Bryn Ellyllon, the hillock of the elves, had been someone's last resting place hundreds of years before. A few beads and a piece of metal had been found (the congregation's eyes gleamed), but there was no sign of anything further, and certainly no treasure (their expressions fell a little).

'But,' he went on, 'of much more importance to us

Christians is the man who *did* dig up a treasure, and was so desirous of owning it, that he sold all he possessed in order to buy that field – which is how we are told we should desire the kingdom of heaven, our true treasure …'

He stood beaming fondly down at them. But the congregation of St Mary's were much more interested in a Mold treasure in a Mold field, and quickly dismissed his words as preachifying.

After the service, the two children and their mother hurried down the slope of Milford Street.

'Well, did you get it all?' she demanded.

Between them they managed to recall most of what the vicar had told them. Sophie pulled her bonnet strings tighter.

'I wish he wouldn't talk so fast,' she said fretfully. 'I start to understand his English, then he says something really quickly and I get lost again.'

'You should go to chapel then,' said Billy provocatively. 'It's all Welsh there.'

'Billy!' said his mother in shocked tones. 'You know we've always gone to St Mary's. I was christened there, and so were all of you children, and we were married there, your father and I, and we shall have a decent Christian burial there, too, God willing, and be laid to rest in the churchyard, same as generations of Mold people.'

'Oh, Mam,' protested Sophie, squeezing her mother's arm. 'Don't go thinking about things like that.'

Billy thought of the bones that had been buried the day before. Had that been a Mold person? Had he or she now really been laid to rest?

As they entered the house their mother's mood

changed and she immediately became more business-like.

'Now *we've* got a different body to dispose of,' she said briskly. It had been decided that Porcyn had reached the desired size, and was to be slaughtered, today. As far back as they could remember, every spring the household fussed over a dear little weaner – only to end the year with the pig-killing. It was part of their lives; in nearly every yard in the street there was a pig or hens to keep a supply of meat going throughout the winter. Now Porcyn's time had come.

Mam had changed from her Sunday best, with its aura of camphor, into her oldest clothes. A wrap-around apron was tied firmly round her waist, and a kerchief hid her long hair.

'Get those good clothes off,' she ordered the children sharply. They knew she was being short-tempered only because of what lay in store for Porcyn – but it had to be.

Sophie and Billy put on their oldest clothes and miserably went out into the yard. They leant over the wall of the sty. Billy patted the sow's bristly back.

'Goodbye, Porcyn,' he said sadly.

'*Ffarwêl, Porcyn, bach*,' said Sophie.

'We still don't know if she's Welsh or English,' said Billy. They had discussed this before.

''Course she's Welsh,' said Sophie. 'She lives in Wales, and she's got a Welsh name.'

'But the farmer at the cattle market said she was born in England.'

'Yes, but she's lived the rest of her life in Wales,' said Sophie. 'She heard only English for the first few months.'

'That's true; we always talk to her in Welsh.'

'Perhaps it depends what her parents were,' suggested Sophie, tickling Porcyn behind the ear.

They were interrupted by the sound of clogs in the yard behind them. Their neighbours, Daniel Timmins, Steffan Owen and Walter Evans, had arrived to help. Daniel, from number 5 Milford Street, worked at the slaughterhouse in Clay Lane, so he already had the expertise and the implements required.

The children backed away from the wall, nodded at the men, and went hastily back into the house. Their mother was collecting buckets, bowls and dishes. The children helped her place them outside the back door, then shut it firmly. They had already shut Rats in upstairs.

They could hear the men's voices in discussion in the yard. There came a roar of 'Steady there!' from Daniel. There was some squealing, some shouting, then some minutes of concentrated silence. Mam came in, flustered, from the yard, placing the largest bowl carefully on the table.

'Keep that fire going,' she instructed the children. 'I'll start the cooking soon.'

Mrs Evans and Mrs Owen bustled in and went out into the yard. They came back bearing large dishes and steaming bowls which they placed on the table. Some of the meat would be salted, some dried, hams boiled, brawn and sausages made, every part of the pig used up – 'until there's nothing left but the squeal,' Mam always said.

She was already busy stirring a large pot on the fire,

full of the ingredients for black puddings.

'Thanks, Mary,' said Mrs Evans and Mrs Owen, each leaving with a large piece of pork on a plate as a return for their help.

That evening Sophie and Mam stored away the meat in the larder. Billy sat at the table with a length of pork loin in front of him. Holding the meat firmly in one hand, with the other he grasped the old bronze candle-stick from the mantelpiece. He rubbed away at the sur-face of the meat with the base of the candlestick, softening the fat skin and scraping away the bristles. It was a task which had become his by family tradition; the square base of the candlestick was wearing thin after years of pressing and scraping.

They went to bed late. Billy's arms were aching from hours of ridding the meat of bristles, but his stomach was full of bread and delicious roast pork. He slept soundly, dreaming of Sophie placing a necklace of golden beads over Porcyn's head.

11

Billy got up every morning now at the same time as his father and brother. He watched them pull on their hard caps and wind their blackened mufflers round their throats. He saw how they set out to the pit, unsmiling, resigned to a life ruled by the start-of-shift hooter and the whims of the deputy.

Then Billy would tie up his own red neckerchief, button his jacket, pat Rats goodbye for the day and leave the house with a wave to his mother. Stepping out eagerly, he would whistle his way up Milford Street, down the High Street and along the Chester road. Passing the flattened top of the Ellyllon tump, he thought of the bones they had buried at the edge of the field. Then he would stride out the rest of the way to Pentre farm.

He called first at the back door of the kitchen. Cook had been in service long ago with his mother, and had taken him under her wing from the start.

'You need feeding up, *bach*,' she said. 'You and that sister of yours, you look too pale by half. Well, there's nothing I can do for her, but at least I can see that *you* get some decent vittles into you.'

Billy was relieved that his mother couldn't hear these comments on her housekeeping; he knew she would be highly mortified.

'Get your teeth into that,' and Cook would hand him a huge wedge of toast spread thickly with beef dripping, or she would push in front of him a dish of fried eggs and a hunk of bread.

After that, Selwyn would come in and give him his orders for the day. These always started with a walk to the fields to bring in the cows for the early milking. As Billy drove them into the byre, Nansi would be waiting with her milking stool.

Billy would line up the cattle and fill the mangers with hay. Nansi would start him on milking one or two of the most docile cows, perhaps Speedwell and

Kingcup. After that, he returned the cattle to the fields. When he came back he helped to lug about full milk buckets and churns, turn the handle of the butterchurn at Nansi's orders, or swill down the dairy. Later he might be sent out to help the shepherd or the plough-man. Billy loved it all – the smell of the byre, the silly gentleness of the cattle, the swish of the milk into the pails, and the constant comings and goings in the yard. No day was ever the same as the last.

He normally saw little of Mr Langford, except on pay day, when Billy stood in line to receive his wages. But one morning the farmer came unexpectedly into the dairy. He had a short smiling conversation with Nansi, then came over to Billy who was scrubbing down the butter-board.

'Enjoying your work here, Billy?'

'Oh, yes, sir.'

'This is a pedigree herd, you know; very well thought of locally.'

'I know, sir.'

'We won an award for Poppy – best three-year-old heifer at the Flintshire Agricultural Society Show. Did you know that?'

'No sir.' But he knew Poppy – a beautiful Jersey heifer with a sweet temper.

'Nansi will tell you more about it – there'll be a bonus for all of you with your wages this week. And we'll want to do even better in the 1834 show, won't we?'

'Oh, *yes*, sir,' beamed Billy.

Some days later, Cook brought the Chester *Chronicle* down into the kitchen.

'It's all in here,' she announced.

'No good to me,' said Nansi. 'You'll have to read it to me.'

They pored over it together. It was in English, but with the help of Cook and Selwyn, they worked out a version they all understood.

The Flintshire Agricultural Society had had a meeting in the Leeswood Arms to award premiums.

'What's that?' asked Nansi.

'Prizes, m'dear, prizes,' said Cook. 'Look here: "To Mr John Langford of Mold for the best three-year-old heifer – a piece of plate, or seven pounds." Fancy!'

'Seven pounds!' echoed Billy. More than Tad earned in six months.

When pay-day came round, Billy always stood at the end of the queue, as befitted the youngest and newest on the payroll. He was left last in the farm office alone with Mr Langford. On this particular day his heart was heavy. He swallowed and forced himself to speak.

'Please could I ask you something, sir?' he whispered.

Mr Langford looked surprised, but said, 'Yes, Billy. But come over here first. I'd like you to see this; I've already shown Nansi and Selwyn.'

He led Billy to a glass-fronted wall cabinet. There, in the place of honour, stood a large silver cup.

'See, Billy, it's inscribed round the edge: "Mr John Langford of Mold, for the best three-year-old heifer, awarded by Flintshire Agricultural Society, 1833." We're very proud of our pedigree herd, you know.'

'Oh, I know, sir.'

The farmer glanced at Billy's enthusiastic face; then he

said suddenly, 'Well, as you're here, you might as well look at this too, seeing as you were there when it was found.'

He pointed to a smaller display cabinet with a glass top. Billy turned to it and gasped when he realized that inside lay the semicircular sheet of embossed gold they had dug up in Bryn Ellyllon. But it had been polished to a gleam the colour of honey. At this sight, Billy's spirits sank even lower.

'I've had to lock it in here, Billy,' said the farmer with a grimace. 'People kept dropping in to look at it, and I reckon one or two pieces have been broken off and went walking! Then the vicar told some of his friends and the news spread abroad. A man from the British Museum in London heard about it and travelled all the way down here to look at it. Now, this very day, I've received a letter from him.'

He pulled a piece of paper from his top pocket and unfolded it.

'They say it's a "peytrel" – part of a horse's armour to protect his forequarters, and it's extremely old. They want to buy it from me for seventy-two pounds! I was flabbergasted, Billy, I don't mind admitting it … absolutely flabbergasted.' Mr Langford seemed to be talking to himself. 'Seventy-two pounds for what we thought was a piece of old scrap, even if it has turned out to be gold … Perhaps it should stay here in Wales … I'll have to think about it … Anyway,' he focused his eyes on Billy again, 'what was your question, boy?'

Billy's fingers clenched and unclenched over the object in his pocket. He kept seeing Drownded's expression as he said solemnly, *Thou shalt not steal*. He felt almost faint with fear. But he had to speak.

'P-please, sir – I've got to give you something. I-I think it may be part of this …' Billy pointed to the glass case. 'Rats – my dog – must have trod on it the day we dug up the body, sir. It cut his pad and I took it out and put it in my pocket unthinking … I'm sorry, sir, I forgot all about it till I found it there again today …'

Mr Langford looked at the dirty piece of metal lying on Billy's outstretched palm. It was a piece about an inch square, its embossed shapes full of dirt. The farmer took one glance and shook his head.

'I've had enough of the whole matter,' he said. 'I've enough to do without men from London, who don't know one end of a cow from another, coming here and suggesting I start digging up all my fields. There's been enough fuss already about the dratted thing – I've already had to have this cabinet made and a padlock fitted, and a pretty penny that cost, I can tell you. Now it's locked in there, and that shall be that, unless or until I sell it to the British Museum.

'So you do what you like with that scrap there, Billy, with my blessing. Now, here's your pay, and you'd better get out sharpish and report to Selwyn, or he'll complain I'm keeping you from your work. Off you go now.'

'Oh, *thank* you, sir!'

Billy felt an enormous burden lift from his shoulders and from his conscience. Nor could he believe the generosity of the bonus Mr Langford had just given him. He counted the coins in his palm yet again: for this one week his pay had been doubled to twelve pence – one whole shilling! He dropped the twelve large coins in his pocket. At the end of the day he ran home planning how he would spend the extra pennies at the coming fair. He felt like a lord.

12
═

Near the end of October, Billy burst into the house one evening. He threw his cap on the peg. His mother came out of the scullery wiping her hands on her apron, her eyes wide, ready for bad news.

'What on earth is it? What's happened?'

'Nothing, Mam – don't always fear the worst. It's the handbills for the fair; they're all over the place.'

Sophie stood behind her mother. Her pale face looked tear-stained.

'What's there to be?'

'The Mold Militia is to give a demonstration of precision drilling – it's all to be held on the rifle range field. And there'll be sideshows – a bearded lady, a sword swallower, a mermaid in a tank of water, a fire eater, a savage African lion, a champion boxer challenging all comers – perhaps Meic would have a go – oh, and lots more.'

'And there'll be pies, toffee apples, gingerbread, and all the rest besides, I suppose,' smiled their mother. 'Well, I shan't bother making any dinner that day. There's something to look forward to, Sophie – think about that, it'll cheer you up.'

Billy's face fell. He glanced anxiously at his sister. He would do anything to prevent her looking like this.

'School, was it?' he asked.

Sophie nodded, her eyes filling with tears.

'I was so scared of forgetting that I couldn't remember one of the verses of a poem. He gave me three strokes of the cane again.'

'Can't she leave, Mam?' demanded Billy. 'She's old enough. She'd soon find work. There's the cotton mill, or she could go into service like you, or –'

'No!' cried Sophie. 'I *want* to learn, I like learning – why should a beastly teacher stop me. I've *got* to go on, there's so much more I want to know.'

Her face was flushed now and her eyes were bright with determination. 'One day *I* shall be a school teacher,' she said. 'I swear it – but I shall use no cane, because I shall see to it that my scholars will enjoy learn-ing.'

The latch rattled and little Jen burst in.

'Guess what – Tad has just come in with a handbill about the fair. It's next week and the militia will be drilling, and –'

The others burst out laughing and the conversation turned to the fair and its delights.

The twenty-second of November arrived at last. It seemed that everyone in Mold somehow found time to go down to the fairground on the rifle range field along-side the Alyn. Only the publicans and shopkeepers stood in their aprons in their shop doorways, watching people making their way down towards the river, sure of extra trade when they returned.

Billy had reported for work as usual, but Mr Langford had sent him off at two o'clock.

'I remember fair days when I was a boy,' he said. 'That'll do for today.'

Billy raced down the Ellyllon meadow past Hen Tŷ – still uninhabited – then along the bank of the Alyn until he came to the stepping stones.

He jumped over them and up the bank onto the flat rifle range field. The place was milling with people. It was just time for the militia's entertainment. They looked splendid in their red and black uniforms. Their bayonets gleamed as they presented arms and performed intricate marching manoeuvres at the roar of command of a fearsome-looking sergeant. The few cavalrymen there looked like young gods, high up on their fine mounts, capes swung over one shoulder, disdainfully ignoring the crowds of onlookers.

The sound of the brass band filled the valley, echoing back from the hills. Round the edge of the field were hundreds of stalls and sideshows. Billy had given his mother sixpence and saved the other six pennies for himself. He jingled them now as he sauntered along in the crisp November air.

He bought a large square of gingerbread for a farthing and munched it. Then he washed it down with half a pint of dandelion and burdock water. Stallholders all round were shouting their wares.

'Guess her weight, young sir,' shouted a voice, and Billy found a squealing piglet dumped into his arms.

Why not? There would need to be a replacement for Porcyn. He estimated the weight of the wriggling body, then gave his name and handed over a halfpenny – only five pence left.

He waved at Sophie who was with a group of school friends, then a voice shouted at him through the crowd.

'Billy!' He recognized Pawl's thin face greeting him through a mouthful of barley sugar. 'Come over here and try the hoop-la, there's some wonderful prizes.'

'Where's the mermaid?' asked Billy looking round. 'I'd like to see a live mermaid. Do you think she's got a tail, a real tail?'

They stood and watched the prize-fighter challenging all comers. He was wearing a black fighting vest and black ankle boots. He stood and flexed his oiled biceps, and the Mold youths looked at him and then at their friends. Was it worth a purse of £5 to risk a black eye – or worse damage – from the Fearsome Fighter of Flint?

Billy and Pawl looked at the livestock: rabbits, chicken, fattened geese and turkeys. There were stalls of fairings, prizes of vases and china dogs to win, aniseed balls, cheese to eat, swing boats to ride on. The military band was still playing, stallholders shouting their wares. A barrel organ player had stationed himself near the tea stall, so that his little monkey could hold out its hand for coins.

It took the two boys two hours to walk round the field twice, and dusk was falling. A bright moon lit up the water meadows and the hills all round the little town. Stallholders packed up by the light of oil lamps they had brought. The militia had already marched back to the barracks. The hurdy gurdy man was still turning the handle wearily. Horses were being unhitched; there was the clink of harness, the snort of horses – the homeward journey was beginning. Occasionally a spine-chilling growl came from the tent where the lion was pacing.

Creaking carts full of chattering folk set out for Llanarmon, Ruthin and Denbigh. Pawl and Billy and other stragglers trudged contentedly back up towards the High Street. There were no lights on this part of the road and they picked their way carefully by the light of the moon.

A few yards ahead of them walked a young lady holding her father's arm. Suddenly he stumbled in a pot-hole and fell awkwardly sideways. He lay there, momentarily dazed. A cart was coming up alongside, and the horse, unable to swerve, was making straight for the man. The young lady screamed, pulling at his coat. Billy recognized Doli in the same moment.

He darted forward.

'Doli!' he shouted, and leapt for her bridle. He yanked on it as hard as he could and she slewed sideways, nearly breaking the shafts of the cart. Pawl and the young lady seized the man and helped him to the side of the road.

'Whatchou think chyou're doing?' said Yanto in a slurred voice. He peered sleepily over the edge of his seat.

'You nearly ran over someone –'

'Oh, itchyou, Billy. Well, I'm shorry, but you shouldn't go waking a fellow up shudden like – I might have fallen off. You know I can tchrust Doli to get me home.'

He sheepishly touched his cap to them, and Doli pulled away again. The man leant against the wall. He was panting heavily. He wiped his forehead and bald head with a trembling hand. Billy retrieved his hat from the roadway and handed it to the young lady.

'Thank you, thank you, young sirs,' said the man. 'I am most grateful. *Mein Gott* – I think I have twisted my foot. Luckily, we live in the next house.'

He put his arm round his daughter's shoulders and leant on her a few more steps up the street. Then he took out a key and opened the door of the jeweller's shop. As the boys anxiously walked behind, they heard him mutter, '*Komm, Kind, schnellstens ins Haus.*'

Then he turned and, still rather shakenly, shook them both by the hand.

'Good night, young sirs, and many, many thanks. I hope you will call into my shop some time soon, so that I may thank you more properly by daylight.'

13

The bell above the shop door tinkled. Pawl pushed Billy into the dark interior, then stumbled in after him. They pulled off their caps and stood nervously staring into the gloom. Neither of them had been inside a jeweller's before – and a foreign newcomer's at that. Mr Bergmann was also a clockmaker. On the walls of the tiny room hung clocks of all descriptions. Pendulums swung, and the air was full of the sound of ticking and an occasional chime.

'Yes?'

There was no one to be seen. They turned their eyes in the direction of the voice. In a corner behind a counter sat a man with a completely bald head. He looked over his glasses at them, his face lit up by the little oil lamp shining onto his work bench. He spoke again, choosing his words slowly.

'May I be of assistance, young sirs?'

Pawl and Billy looked at one another. Suddenly the man's expression changed.

'Ah, it is my young friends of the other night. How pleased I am to make your acquaintance once more.'

He stood up and came round the counter to shake their hands again.

Billy smiled and timidly gathered together what English he could.

'We hope you are well?'

'Oh, yes, no bones are broken. I am so grateful. You were so quick to think.'

Pawl and Billy had rehearsed what Billy was to say. Now he stammered, 'I would l-like a ring to give to my s-sister.'

Mr Bergmann looked a little startled, but answered politely, 'Yes. We have many fine rings. May I show some to you?'

'I want a ring, but I would like you to make it, if you please,' said Billy carefully. 'I have gold to make it.'

The bald man adjusted his spectacles and examined the scrap of embossed metal which Billy was holding out to him.

'Yes, it is truly gold,' he agreed. 'It is good quality. Perhaps from South Wales?'

He looked up questioningly.

'It's not stolen,' said Billy quickly, 'you can ask Mr John Langford of Pentre farm – he knows all about it.' He went on. 'I want a ring for my sister. She has small fingers –' He held out one of his hands. '– Smaller than this.'

Mr Bergmann nodded.

'Plain? Or would you wish a pattern?'

Billy had thought about this. He wanted this to be very special.

'Can you make it in a plait pattern?'

The jeweller looked bewildered. He didn't understand.

'A plait?' He made it sound like *plet*.

Billy looked round. How could he explain? He held out his two hands and intertwined the fingers. 'Like this.'

'Ah.' The man nodded, then called into the back room.

'Liesel? *Komm her, Liebchen.*'

There was the sound of footsteps, and a girl of about the boys' age came round the dark red curtain in the doorway. She was dressed in blue, with a little black velvet bodice. Her blonde hair was wound round her head in a smooth plaited crown. The man stood up and put his arm round her. He pointed to her hair and looked at Billy.

'A plait?' he asked. 'So?'

'Yes, yes.' Billy nodded vigorously. Both boys stared

at Liesel. She was so neat and so pretty. She smiled at them, then bobbed a curtsy at her father, 'Papa', and disappeared behind the curtain again.

'My daughter Liesel,' said the man proudly. 'Is she not beautiful? But she speaks little English. Now we have left Switzerland and come to live here in Wales, she must practise much with her governess.'

'Welsh?' asked Pawl.

'No, that is too difficult,' answered her father sadly. 'And all customers understand at least a little English, so she will learn English to help me in the shop.'

He became businesslike again and looked at Billy.

'So – you wish a ring with a plait pattern? I shall make it for you.'

Billy hesitated. This was the difficult part.

'Can I pay you a penny a week until it's paid for?'

The jeweller smiled.

'That will not be necessary. I shall make a small ring like a plait, and I shall make it gladly because Liesel and I are grateful.'

Billy's face lit up. His English was unable to rise to the occasion, but he beamed in reply. Pawl slapped him on the shoulder, equally pleased.

'How old is your sister?' asked the jeweller suddenly.

'Eleven.'

'Like my Liesel. What is she called?'

'Sophie.'

The man tried it out, 'Sophie – that rings well. I shall have the work ready in eight days. Bring your sister when you return after eight days. Speak to your parents about the matter. Perhaps your Sophie will learn to know my Liesel and they can speak together.'

'Sophie speaks Welsh. Her English is … not perfect.'

Mr Bergmann brightened.

'Then perhaps she can sit with Liesel and the governess – and they all speak English together? My Liesel needs a friend.'

The boys left the little shop and stood on the High Street, looking at one another disbelievingly.

'From Switzerland,' said Pawl. 'Did you see that enormous picture of mountains behind him?'

Billy's thoughts were elsewhere.

'She's called Liesel,' he breathed. 'With a governess! Just wait till I tell Mam and Sophie. Wouldn't it be wonderful if they could become friends?'

14

It was impossible for Billy to keep things secret. He told his mother, knowing that she would tell his father. Sophie listened to Billy's pleas on her behalf in despairing silence.

'Will you ask him, Mam?'

'I have asked him.'

'What did he say?'

'He said, how could the daughter of a pitman sit with a young lady and her governess?'

'But Mam – Sophie's the same age as the young … as Miss Liesel. They could be friends. And Sophie needs something like this. She's always moping and sad. She really wants to learn, but she can't if she's not encouraged.'

His mother sighed.

'It's out of the question, Billy. They're a different class to us. How could we afford to pay a governess?' She pushed wisps of hair back from her face. 'Come Sophie, get those things set on the table.'

Billy persisted.

'But Mr Bergmann made it sound like an invitation.'

He looked earnestly from his mother to Sophie. 'I don't think he meant it to cost you anything.'

'But the books, and the clothes …' His mother shook her head. 'She's a young lady from what you say. Look at your sister – how could Sophie mix with her?'

Billy looked at Sophie in her darned black wool stockings, scuffed buttoned boots, the white – not so white – apron which covered her grey dress, and the long untidy plait hanging down over one thin shoulder. Her face looked drawn. Billy tried once more.

'But Mam, you will ask him again, won't you?' he urged.

Sophie looked so woebegone that her mother was sorry for her.

'I'll see,' she said. 'If I find the right moment …'

Next evening, when Tad and Meic had come in and had washed, they all sat down to their meal. There was silence for a while as they ate.

'Another dumpling, Gwilym?'

'I will. They're good,' said Tad.

'You, too, Meic. They'll line your stomach and keep

out the cold in that nasty old pit.'

After the meal Tad sat down on the settle near the range. He filled his pipe and lit it with a spill touched into flame on the glowing coals.

'Cup of tea, Gwilym?' asked Mam.

He nodded. Sophie undid his pit boots. He sat in his stockinged feet, puffing contentedly and gazing into the fire. Rats came over and sprawled against him. Sophie and Billy looked at their mother. Surely now was the moment.

'Gwilym,' she began, 'you remember I told you about that Mr Bergmann, the Swiss gentleman Billy rescued from the runaway horse and cart?'

'And then went into his shop seeking a trinket for Sophie?'

'Yes, yes, I explained all that to you. Mr Langford said Billy could, and the Swiss gentleman said he would do the work gladly for Billy, he was so grateful …'

Tad grunted.

'The Swiss gentleman. Yes, well, what about him?'

'Have you thought any more about it?'

'About what?'

He was being awkward.

'About Sophie getting to know the girl?'

'How can Sophie get to know a girl who speaks nothing but Swiss?'

'German, Tad,' Billy put in.

'German! That's worse.'

'Like King George and King William, Tad.'

'Exactly – German – all bad or mad …'

'*No*, Tad. Mr Bergmann was a very pleasant gentleman. He said I was to make sure and ask my parents, and of course Sophie would be chaperoned, the governess would be there the whole time.'

'Oh, please, Tad,' pleaded Sophie.

She knelt on the floor beside him. 'Mayn't I just go and meet her?'

Meic was spooning sugar into his tea. Now he spoke for the first time.

'Can't do any harm, can it? Let Mam go with them. She'll soon see if it's a genuine offer.'

They looked at their elder brother gratefully.

'They live just by the Cross,' said Billy eagerly. 'You know, that tiny shop near to the baker's. We could call on Saturday. That's when he said I could … could call again.' He didn't go into details about the ring, wanting to surprise Sophie as much as possible. '*Please*, Tad.'

Their father blew out a long stream of smoke. There was an anxious silence.

'I suppose Meic's right,' he said at last. 'It can do no harm. Your mother will talk to the gentleman, then I'll decide.'

The conversation turned to other matters. Meic wanted to talk. He and Beti had decided to wed in the new year.

'We've seen a place to rent in a house behind Glanrafon – two ground floor rooms, privy in the yard, running water, nice and modern – not cheap, but we shall manage.'

Billy was disappointed.

'Didn't you want Hen Tŷ down beyond Bryn Ellyllon?' he asked. 'I go past it every day. They say the rent is dirt cheap. It's still empty.'

'Yes, and derelict,' said Meic. 'We told you, it's haunted, boy. There's no way Beti wants to bring up a family in a place like that.'

'But it's big,' said Billy, 'and feels nice – much better than two rooms behind Glanrafon.'

'Beti's made up her mind,' said Meic. So they knew that was to be that.

15
=

The next afternoon, without saying anything to anyone, Mam called in at the jeweller's. She reported everything to Tad that evening.

'The Swiss gentleman treated me very kindly,' she said, 'and the young lady, Miss Liesel, is charming. She said she so wanted to meet Sophie; I think she would be a lovely companion for her. She took me into the back parlour and introduced me to the governess, a Miss Bell from Northwich in Cheshire. She seemed a nice young person, and made me tea and I had a slice of seed cake. There was a cloth of Swiss lace and best bone china; it's a long time since I've seen such an elegant afternoon tea table.'

Mam's eyes were bright. It had been quite an adventure. She still had her best shawl round her shoulders.

'Well, Gwilym?' she ventured.

Sophie and Billy looked at Tad. Eventually he shrugged.

'Well, yes, Mary, if you're set on it,' he said. 'I suppose

it may help Sophie's prospects later – as long as you don't get ideas above your station, girl. Perhaps it's time I came and talked to the foreigner myself.'

At the end of the week, Tad accompanied Billy and Sophie – all well scrubbed and brushed – down to the jeweller's. They entered the tiny shop and waited for their eyes to grow accustomed to the gloom. Sophie looked round astonished at the ticking clocks and the cabinets full of silver plate and fine jewellery.

Mr Bergmann was delighted to see them. He stood up and came round the counter to bow over Tad's hand, then to greet Sophie and Billy.

'Liesel,' he called. 'Miss Sophie is here.'

He turned to them.

'She has been counting the days until she might learn to know Miss Sophie,' he said. 'It will be good for her to have a friend of her own age.'

He began to talk to Tad. Liesel came in and shyly held out her hand to Sophie.

'I am pleased to meet you,' she said carefully. 'Please excuse me, my English is poor. So it will be good to share my studies.'

'Oh, no,' said Sophie, 'it will be good for me. I want to learn, but I do not like school. I would rather be at home with my family.'

'You have a big family?'

'Me, Billy here, my parents, Meic our big brother – oh, and Rats.'

'Rats?' Liesel looked puzzled.

Sophie laughed.

'Rats is a dog.'

'A dog! You have a dog – oh, Papa, *Fräulein Sophie hat einen Hund* – Miss Sophie has a dog!'

Liesel's father smiled at her fondly. 'Yes, and I am learning that Mr Bellis is a coalminer. When I was young, Mr Bellis, I too was a miner, but in a silver mine – and so I became interested in working the metal. Even my name, you see, "Bergmann", means miner! We have much in common, Mr Bellis.'

Tad was already looking more relaxed.

'But now,' said the jeweller, 'I have something for young Mr Bellis here.'

Billy looked round, then realized that meant himself. Mr Bergmann handed him a small blue box. Billy received it with sudden excitement. He turned to Sophie and opened it in front of her. Inside, on a pad of black velvet, lay a gleaming gold ring.

'Ohhh,' breathed Sophie.

They all watched as she slipped it onto her middle finger. The plaited pattern shone in the light of the jeweller's lamp. The gleam of gold drew attention to Sophie's white hands.

'It's beautiful,' she whispered. 'I've never owned anything so beautiful in my life. Oh, Billy, *thank* you.'

She turned to give her brother a grateful kiss and hugged him as though she would squeeze the breath from his body. The others all beamed. Billy's face shone.

'Thanks to Mr Bergmann too,' he said. 'The ring is perfect. You've made it exactly as I hoped.'

The jeweller bowed.

'I thank you, Mr Billy. It was a privilege to handle such gold. It was a delight to work with. But now, please, come, all of you, into our little parlour. I shall introduce Miss Bell, and I invite you to drink tea with us. Thus, *hoffentlich*, will begin a long acquaintance.'

Mold, North Wales

Later This Year

It was five minutes to ten on a July morning. Part of Tesco's car park had been roped off. Prospective customers stared towards the shady side near the wall, to see what was going on, and why a crowd was gathering. Mrs Evans the headteacher was there with Mr Salmon and his class. The manager of Tesco's Mold branch was there, chatting to various VIPs from Head Office. Some of the off-duty staff had come out, as well as proud parents, two local reporters, a press photographer, and a news team from S4C television.

Although people were talking and laughing, all eyes kept turning towards the long wall. Its plastered surface was completely hidden by the brilliantly coloured scenes painted on it.

The children kept asking one another, 'Doesn't it look marvellous?' and 'Isn't it ace now it's finished?' moving from foot to foot in a mixture of embarrassment and delight in their own handiwork.

A golden ribbon had been strung along the middle of the length of the wall. To the far left was the first scene – the Clwydian hills in prehistoric times, covered in dense forests, where animals roamed. Next came a picture of a goldsmith fashioning the torc, surrounded by admiring villagers. This was William's work. He had been so careful when he painted the torc, using gold paint for the first time in his life.

The next scene was of sloping fields round Mold.

Bishop Germanus and his men were preparing to do battle in the year 420.

A thousand years later St Mary's Church was being built. Medieval builders were climbing up ladders to work on the half-finished walls. Some of the workmen were sitting nearby, carving animals on stones to decorate the walls.

Next on the mural were four portraits. The first was Richard Wilson, the artist, painting in the Welsh countryside. The second was Robert Davies, a young doctor from Mold, on the deck of a boat with Captain\ off Tahiti.

The third was William's imagined portrait of Great-great-great-grandfather Billy as a boy, with a group of other Mold people, looking at the piece of gold torc they had just dug up. The fourth portrait was the writer Daniel Owen, working as an apprentice in the Mold tailor's shop.

The next scenes showed soldiers drilling outside Mold Barracks in the First World War. Then followed Mold men and women in the uniforms of various regiments in the Second World War. The children had brought in family photos to copy, to make sure details were accurate.

There followed paintings of some well-known buildings in Mold, including a scene in a pantomime taking place on stage at Theatr Clwyd. The last section portrayed people of the town today – a well-known butcher, baker, policeman, clergyman, a market stallholder, the town crier, the mayor – and a uniformed Tesco employee at the check-out. And forming a border at the top and bottom of the wall were pictures of the flowers, trees, birds, animals and human faces that the children thought might have been seen in their part of North Wales throughout history.

More people were coming over to join the spectators, exclaiming and pointing as they recognized scenes or people.

'I had no idea it was going to be like this,' murmured a voice in William's ear. It was his mother who had taken the morning off work to be there. 'No wonder it took so much research. It's absolutely stunning. I must go and congratulate Mr Salmon on your class's work.'

One or two people were beginning to look up at Tesco's clock – nearly ten past ten. Then the mayor of Mold, dignified in his chain of office, climbed onto a low platform and tapped the microphone which had been placed ready.

'*Croeso*, ladies and gentlemen, *cyfeillion*. This is one of the most interesting and delightful tasks it has ever been my pleasure to undertake. Many congratulations to Mr Salmon and his class for their amazing work. It will now be even more of a pleasure to visit Tesco's. (Laughter from the supermarket staff.)

'The research, the design, the quality of the painting, the brilliant colours, and the vision of the whole project, have all been realized at a level of excellence which is amazing in children so young. We are proud of you, children!' (Much applause from the spectators.)

The mayor went on. 'I've already walked up and down past this mural three times, and I learn something more about our local history every time. The scenes and people depicted are just some of the constituent parts of life here in north-east Wales. At some times those places were under Welsh domination, some times under English. Some of those people spoke Welsh, some spoke English, some spoke both; some settlers in prehistoric times came from far away, and spoke a language we wouldn't recognize at all.'

'I can see people here today' – he gestured at the crowd – 'whom I know well. Some were born Welsh, some have achieved Welshness, and some have had Welshness thrust upon them.' (Laughter.) 'But what they and we all share is our humanity; we are all members of the human tribe. And that is what these children have tried to portray: our pride in ourselves as members of the human race in our own small corner of the world – what a wonderful achievement!'

A burst of cheers and clapping greeted his words. He bent towards the golden ribbon. He felt in his pockets and his smile faded. Tesco employees looked round.

'Scissors, scissors,' they muttered to one another.

Mr Salmon threw a quick glance in William's direction and pulled from his pocket a dark red Swiss army knife. He nicked open the small pair of scissors and handed it politely to the mayor.

The mayor's smile brightened and he bent to the golden ribbon once more and cut. The two pieces of ribbon leapt away to right and left, and the crowd applauded enthusiastically.

The reporters had been checking their pocket tape recorders; the photographer was taking pictures of the mayor and other VIPs, with the wall as a background.

The TV camera crew came over to Mr Salmon and the children.

'We'd like pictures of you all against different scenes of the mural, please,' said a man in a green pullover who seemed to be in charge. 'Can you stroll up and down, chatting naturally?'

The children smirked self-consciously, but walked along from one end of the mural to the other, pointing out particular places that they had painted. Mr Salmon took the opportunity to murmur to William, 'This would seem to be an auspicious occasion,' and handed over the Swiss army knife. He then added sternly, 'Not, strictly *not*, for school use, William.'

'Oh no, sir, thank you, sir,' said William, and kept the precious knife clutched in his hand in his jacket pocket.

The mayor came up to Mr Salmon with the TV cameraman following close behind.

'They're looking for new designs for a set of stamps featuring Wales,' he said. 'I'm going to recommend scenes from the mural. It's just what we need, young people's work.'

A month later William and his mother moved into the Old House. The moving men had some difficulty, as there was no road to the house. However, with great good humour they brought the furniture piece by piece along the little path between the houses and the rugby pitch. One of them was a local man who promised to help with the garden. He came round the following weekend with his scythe, his cousin, and his cousin's rotavator. Within a day, the nettles were slain, and the soil turned over. William's mother was in her element.

'I've all sorts of plans for the garden,' she said to William happily. 'I'm going to put new raspberry canes over there, where there were a few already. I'm going to plant herbs over there, where the mint was taking over. And I think I'll grow honeysuckle up that sunny wall there, and plant some roses next to it, where that white stone is.'

'Oh, the one with R scratched on it?'

'Yes, it's odd, isn't it? It's almost like a little headstone – perhaps for a pet or something.'

They sat on the back doorstep, each with a mug of tea, musing. The Alyn trickled along, a few metres below them. Jet splashed along by the bank, sniffing for water rats.

'By the way,' said William's mother, 'your Mr Salmon's quite nice, isn't he? Not a bit like you make him out to be. I bumped into him in the market and invited him for tea on Sunday. He's offered to come and advise me on renewing some of the woodwork – says he's an expert on window-sills. Did you know that?'

William gave a hoot of laughter, and fell over backwards, unable to stop chortling. Jet galloped up to join the fun and threw himself onto William for a friendly wrestling session.

'That's enough, you two,' said William's mother. 'William – come and help me plant this rosemary bush I bought at the market. Will you dig the hole? I'll bring the watering can and the bush.'

'I hope Sophie would have approved of where we're going to plant it,' said William.

His mother didn't answer directly. Then she remarked, almost to herself, 'Rosemary for remembrance.'

The evening sun was slanting sideways against the distant trees as they walked over to the herb garden. It was very quiet. William carried the spade.

'Here?' He began to cut out a deepish hole. His mother poured in some of the water. Suddenly she crouched down.

'What's that, shining in the water?'

She lowered her hand into the hole and felt about. She lifted something up to peer at it, then stood up and held it out to William.

'Look –'

'A ring,' breathed William. 'A little gold ring.'

He took it and rubbed it on his jeans. He held it out to his mother.

'It's got a sort of pattern all round, like a plait.'

With growing excitement, his mother took out her hanky to clean it.

Something caught William's eyes. He looked up suddenly. A man, whose upper body dazzled like gold in the light of the setting sun, was walking slowly up the distant slope. He stood for a moment, as though looking at William in recognition, then merged into the hillside and disappeared.

Mold, North Wales

c. 3,000 Years Ago

They walked slowly down the side of the hill from the village towards the river. The six litter-bearers, all blood-brothers of Pendefig, slowly led the way. The litter was draped with a single piece of fine white woollen cloth, and on it lay Pendefig's body.

Whitehands walked behind the litter. Little Gwil walked by her side, clinging to her skirt. On his other side padded Glew, the wolf-hound. Gwil clutched a handful of the dog's rough grey hair; it was familiar and comforting.

The boy's expression was solemn, for he knew he would never see his father again after today – and besides, it disturbed him to see his mother cry.

Whitehands was exhausted after nearly two weeks of nursing Pendefig. It had happened so quickly. She had been weaving – the same piece of cloth on which Pendefig now lay – when she heard the sound of the men's voices returning from their hunting trip. She picked up Gwil and ran to the door of the hut to see what they had brought.

But it was no stag or wild ox the others were half-dragging, half-carrying into the village – it was their young chieftain, Pendefig. His tunic was wet with a large red stain.

'Wild boar,' said her brother, Heliwr, briefly. 'It's taken three hours to get back. He's lost a lot of blood.'

They helped him in and laid him down on the bed. When Whitehands cut away his tunic and shift, she gasped at the extent of the wound. The tusk had torn deeply into his flesh at stomach level, and the gash was still bleeding. Gwil watched from a dark corner; he didn't want to be sent outside with the other children, he wanted to watch.

Quickly, Whitehands brought water to wash the wound, then she packed it with leaves and cloths. Pendefig lay there, pale and shivering, even under the fur covers. Suddenly, Gwil ran over and tried to climb onto his father to play, as he often did. When White-hands snatched him off, he tried to struggle back.

'Let him, let him,' whispered Pendefig, and managed to smile at Gwil.

The men of the tribe came in to watch. They told and retold how the enormous boar had appeared as though from nowhere, charging past them from the bushes, then suddenly wheeling viciously on Pendefig and slic-ing at him with its tusks. He had managed to send his spear into the beast's flank before he collapsed.

Eventually the blood stopped flowing. But the wound did not heal, even though Doeth, the Wise Woman of the tribe, brought mistletoe, bloodwort, and other herbs, and helped Whitehands to apply them.

The flesh round the wound became red and swollen. Pendefig was in great pain. The wound turned black and poisonous. He became delirious, and tossed and shouted for two days and nights, in a frenzied boar hunt. Then he fell unconscious, and Whitehands knew they had lost him. He had gone to join their ancestors.

The men came to the hut to pay their respects to their dead leader.

'We shall go back there and kill the boar,' they promised fiercely.

Whitehands shrugged, and her eyes filled.

'What use is the tusker to me?' she asked, looking down at Pendefig's body.

Doeth and the other women came into the hut. They helped Whitehands prepare the body for burial. They washed and anointed Pendefig and dressed him in his softest goatskin robe.

'Now the gold cape,' said Whitehands. The women stared at her.

'But it is your son's now,' said old Doeth in consternation. 'He has inherited it.'

The other women nodded; sons always inherited; this was how it had always been.

'No,' said Whitehands firmly. 'My son shall wear whatever he wishes when he is old enough to become chieftain. But Pendefig is to make his last journey in his ceremonial cape, as befits a prince.'

They were silent, and she fetched a bundle wrapped in softest red cloth. They watched her long white fingers slowly unwrap it, then gasped when they saw the cape again. The light gleamed on the hundreds of patterns embossed in the glowing gold. She ran her fingertips over the lines of raised circles and ovals which went round the cape.

'He paid ten fine axe-heads and a score of boars' tusks for that gold,' she said proudly, 'When he was away hunting in the south, far beyond the mountains.'

'Yes,' said Doeth, 'I remember Gof working away for days on these patterns in the smithy. He was so determined it should be his most perfect piece of work. We all gathered round to watch, and no one dared speak.'

'Yes,' said Whitehands, smiling. 'Then when Gof finished, I tied a doeskin thong in every single one of those holes to make a fringe. And how handsome Pendefig looked when he put it on for the first time!'

Her lip trembled.

The women fitted the cape carefully round Pendefig's shoulders.

'See how snugly it fits the curve of his upper arms,' said old Doeth admiringly.

'Yes, it was measured and made for him alone,' said Whitehands softly.

They finished their task and stood back to look at him – his thick black eyebrows; his face, waxy as tallow; his long black hair, which Whitehands had carefully brushed. The gold cape gleamed round his shoulders and chest. Old Doeth nodded her white head in satisfaction as they gazed at him.

'Perfect,' she said.

'No', said Whitehands suddenly. She pulled her amber necklace over her head.

'He shall take these with him. He bought them for me from a northerner whose language we didn't understand – do you remember that trader, Doeth? – how we laughed as the two of them made signs, trying to barter with fur, then antlers, then ivory. In the end the northerner took a bronze dagger for them, but Pendefig still said it was a bargain.'

Whitehands held the beads up in the sunshine at the door of the hut. They glowed orange and yellow against the light. Then she slipped them round Pendefig's head and arranged them on the gold cape.

'So he will have something to remember me by,' she thought, 'on his journey.'

Now she reached down for Gwil's hand and held it tightly as they followed the litter. Behind walked the rest of the tribe. They were nearly all related to herself or Pendefig. The bards had started the burial music – a new chant about a young prince killed by a giant boar. Their singing always moved her. She tried hard not to think of things inside her, only of things outside – the splashing river, the sunshine on the water, those yellow flowers in the grass near the burial chamber.

The grave was ready. They had moved aside the entrance stone. Ashes of other members of the family had already been buried there in red clay pots. Pendefig was to be the last. His body was not to be burnt. He was to be laid to rest as befitted a great prince. Then the bone chamber would be closed, earth and stones piled over it. It would stand as a memorial to their family, and to Pendefig the chief, for ever.